# THE INCURABLE

*by the same author*

UP THE JUNCTION

TALKING TO WOMEN

POOR COW

NELL DUNN

# *The Incurable*

JONATHAN CAPE
THIRTY BEDFORD SQUARE LONDON

FIRST PUBLISHED 1971



JONATHAN CAPE LTD,
30 BEDFORD SQUARE, LONDON WC1

ISBN 0 224 00516 2

Printed and bound in Great Britain by
Richard Clay (The Chaucer Press), Ltd,
Bungay, Suffolk

Warm thanks to Anne Ashberry for letting me quote at length from her lovely book: *Gardens on a Higher Level*; also to Robin Williamson and Mike Heron of The Incredible String Band for letting me use the words of 'The Water Song'.

The quotation on p. 9 from 'Not So Far as the Forest' by Edna St Vincent Millay (*Collected Poems*, Harper & Row, copyright 1939, 1967 by Edna St Vincent Millay and Norma Millay Ellis) is reproduced by permission of Norma Millay Ellis.

FOR MY SONS

Poor passionate thing,
Even with this clipped wing how well you flew! –
            though not so far as the forest.

Rebellious bird, warm body foreign and bright,
Has no one told you? – Hopeless is your flight
Towards the high branches.

Edna St Vincent Millay

# PART ONE

It happened like this. We were in the house. It was early morning, about six, I heard the central heating start up like the engine of a small pleasure-boat. Jonny started to cry. Ricci got out of bed and fell over on the yellow hair-cord. 'Fuck,' he said.

He sat on the bed. I looked at him over the edge of the sheet. 'He's ugly,' I thought.

'I can see everything double, Maro. What's happening?'

I left him there – I hate ill men. I went and fetched Jonny. When I came back he was being sick on the floor, shivering and crying.

I fetched a pink sponge and started to wipe his face. He fell backwards, shaking and retching, like some hideous stranded fish. His body had gone mad.

Then it was the blue electric ambulance in the dark damp dawn – skidding over the brown leaves, through the hospital grounds. 'I'm in pain,' he said.

He was in a white cotton night-dress, lying on a trolley, holding my hand tight, tight.

Three nights ago he talked of death. 'I've had this feeling for about a year, that death is near me, that I'm going to die soon – it is like a Chinese poem. I am going on a long journey and I must look carefully for the last time on the people I love.'

They took him to have his anaesthetic; the door swung

shut. Once I was allowed in, when Seth had his tonsils out – he hung on to my hand while they held a Teddy-bear up to his face and gas came out of the Teddy-bear's mouth – but it wasn't strong enough and the anaesthetist produced a black mask instead. He screamed and tried to push it away and desperately struggled to get into my arms and then shut his eyes quite suddenly and fell backwards. Grown-ups don't fight so hard ...

In the waiting-room, the physiotherapist was showing a forty-year-old, red-cheeked mother how to exercise her paralysed baby's twisted legs. The woman, clumsy, heavy, watches, tries to smile, and suddenly collapses, hand to mouth, on to her chair. The dainty physiotherapist fetches a cup of water, the mother looks up. 'I suddenly felt sick, I don't know why, it must be because I skipped breakfast.'

*   *   *

I sat down in Sister's office. Sister handed me some coffee. The consultant had a pen in his hand; he sat behind Sister's desk, looking at me. He was young and wore a tweed suit. How nice to be married to him.

'Now I expect you want to know exactly what's wrong with your husband and what we're going to do about it.'

She looked up into his eyes. He was looking at her, he was worried she might cry. But 'Yes' she said in a very bright voice and she wondered if he were married already.

Sister's office in the maternity ward – cups of Ovaltine with the night nurses – the smell of nipple cream – the rattle of traffic in the main road – the days spreading into nights – the nurse with the thermometer – the cup of warm, sweet tea – the white bundle of baby ...

'We believe your husband has multiple sclerosis. It is fairly unusual to have such a sudden onset although in about 17 per cent of cases the symptoms do develop in a matter of minutes.'

They gave her a different drug last time – injected into her leg; it was marvellous – she saw right into her body, the red slippery guts and Jonny struggling through it all to get out.

The consultant was asking her some questions – he was concerned but he was trying to keep an optimistic calmness in his voice. 'This is an odd disease – he may be home in a week with the vast majority of symptoms altogether disappearing ...'

She tried to pay attention to what he was saying – she found it difficult to follow – she felt vaguely elated as if something important had happened – a new baby? No it wasn't that.

* * *

The next day she woke late so Tim and Seth didn't go to school. Instead she got bowls of Rice Krispies and brought them back to bed where the little boys were romping. Jonny spilt his on his bare leg and started to cry.

I licked it off and he laughed.

I played a Dylan record and danced about the floor; they danced too, leaping on one leg, falling over and laughing. I did a Yoga exercise – a difficult one. You have to balance on your coccyx and stick your legs in the air hanging on to your ankles. We all tried and fell over and Jonny rolled about the floor giggling, his small pink bottom smelling of pee from the soaking nappy I had just peeled off.

* * *

She pours green pine into the bath and climbs in with Jonny. She lies back and he lies back against her chest, head on her shoulder, soft feet against her thigh. He holds up her hand. 'Tom Thumb, Peter Pointer, Miggleman Tall,' he whispers and the whisper echoes in the steam. She shuts her eyes and feels the weight of his body as he moves his feet in the lapping water. 'Ruby ring, baby small.' He holds up his own tiny pink finger.

Later she went to the hospital. Ricci was in a small ground-floor ward with two other men. His bed was by the window, a sparrow sat on the sill. 'Careful,' he said to Maro. 'You'll frighten the sparrow.' The sparrow flew away. 'The nurses are nice here,' he said. 'They're pretty. I like spending the day in bed. I don't know why I ever used to bother to get up.' His face was very white and there were black circles under his eyes. Every now and then his leg jerked in the air.

'Can't you stop your leg doing that?'

He laughed. 'It looks so funny – it's a spasm – it's common with this disease.'

The nurse who had been fiddling with the man opposite suddenly began to pump her arm up and down and Maro saw the man rise out of bed and swing through the air. It was like a circus. 'Stop, nurse,' he yelled. 'My slipper's fallen off.' His foot was blue and swollen like a baboon's behind. Of course they wouldn't have had a nurse handy in the circus.

'That's the hoist,' said Ricci.

But what about going up hills in Scotland? she wondered ... Walking over those fine unending hills. He wanted to touch the snow which lay only at the top of the farthest mountain. I made him turn back. I was exhausted. We lay on the hillside with the wind, a few drops of rain and a racing sun. For a while we walked hand in hand, his warm hand. 'You are the mother of my child,' he said. I lay in his arms all night.

Maro loved the hospital. She sat by Ricci's bed, the hours drifted by, every now and then she went to the canteen and bought a bag of crisps and a cup of tea and a packet of fruit pastilles. She liked listening to people around her talking.

'I'm impotent and my wife likes dancing. She's taken to going dancing regularly and I don't know if she's formed any attachments. Being impotent doesn't help a marriage work.' Maro was surprised. She looked at the speaker – he was grey and twisted like an old ivy growth in a winter forest.

'One night I lay in the snow for an hour and a half unable to get up outside my own front door. Luckily a neighbour noticed me when she put the cat out.'

It must have been beautiful, the snow and the stars in an inky night and the cold snow on his face.

Going back down the corridor an old woman in a brown dressing-gown stops her and points to a trolley pushed against the side of the wall. 'They all know what that's for, that's their last ride out, when they take the final curtain, the last bow ...'

The curtains of night pinned back by the stars.

* * *

Maro bought a canary. She held out her hand for the change, watching his face to try and discover when she should close it. She tried to understand what he was saying. 'Thirteen and six,' he said, putting a shilling in her hand. Why should he call a shilling piece 'thirteen and six'? He added a two-shilling piece and called it 'fifteen and six'. Did the canary sing? – If it really sang then it was worth being cheated but she wasn't sure she was being cheated. 'One pound,' he said. She looked at him. He was grimy, hunched, the pet shop smelling of musty animal and bird-seed and blocks of red frozen dog's-meat and the cages of twittering, cheeping, blue, yellow and green birds, cheeping not singing. Would her canary sing? Sing to the children?

She balanced the small cage on the pram and pushed it into Woolworth's. 'Sweeties, sweeties,' sang Jonny, jigging up and down.

The sweets had beautiful names: Palace Delights, Playtime Drops, Silver Mints, Nut Bits, Licorice Humbugs. She bought some Royale Assortment.

On the next counter were some apricot and blue nylon panties, hanging on a turning stand. She spun it round, blue bikini tricot briefs, lace-edged, and pale green slips. A vague feeling of jealousy came over her: kissing and love and frolicking intimacy in apricot petticoats, a feeling of jealousy like when the girl on television had said all she wanted to do for her honeymoon was to spend a week in bed.

Everyone seemed to be doing things a long way off ... making sense of their lives, taking delight in their plump babies and week-end shopping.

When she was seventeen, walking down the road, her and herself, her hand inside her blouse, feeling her soft breast rising and falling as she walked and then seeing buses and people and houses and the whole of her responding with joy. A happiness when she woke in the mornings, a waking with joy one winter when the ice was that hard it was breaking the branches of the trees.

Perhaps there was a time long ago when mothers and children swam together in golden water and dried their bodies in the sun and she remembered in Mexico by the river the mothers bent over flat stones while their naked sons, and daughters in thin white slips, swam near by, black hair spread on water. Why was it all so difficult to get it together – to get in touch with the babies? She remembered their births, such shattering moments. Those moments of total joy got fewer. She felt herself getting remoter, more and more detached; she would drift through the days, pleased when five o'clock came and the children seemed stiller, quieter in the evenings, there was the bath and the cereal upstairs and the bed and the raft to have a gentle sleep together; but more and more she failed to understand what it was all about, these babies, why were they eating up her heart? How did she ever have the strength to love a man when they ate every ounce of love and still left her so lonely?

She lay upstairs and listened to them quarrelling and saw the wreck of her bedroom – the ink spilled over her desk and the paper-clips tumbled over the floor, scattered like bright stars over the carpet – and the screams of the baby approaching up the stairs, louder and louder the crescendo and the enraged voice 'Mama, Mama' totally merciless like the sea in storm.

Jonny came into the room and saw her purse. He stopped crying and picked it up. Carefully he pulled out all the money – pound notes and new crisp five-pound notes were scattered on the floor round his small bare feet. He started to crunch and crumple them in his hands and then drop them in a heap on the ground. She looked at him. 'I mustn't let him do that but if I stop him he'll scream again.' 'No, Jonny, no,' she said half-heartedly. He looked at her and began to tear up a note very slowly, he tore it across and then looked at her again, chattering a little like some small animal.

She held out her hand. 'Give them to me.' He gave a

little squeal and turned his back on her, his hands full of notes. She came up to him and bent down and tried to take them from him. He screamed and pulled at them, his face red, his toes curling round dug into the carpet. Inside her chest she felt a desperate churning at the noise. She felt sick. What did it matter if he tore the money up as long as he didn't scream, it was the screaming that destroyed her. The screaming that made her feel sick, mad, disintegrated. It would take him at least four minutes to tear up fifty pounds and during that time he would be quiet – perhaps that was quite cheap for silence – silence was so beautiful – or was it too much to pay – she didn't know. She was filled with a feeling of inadequacy. She just didn't know. She looked in her *Commercial Man's Guide* (she had bought it in Smith's that morning) but it was all to do with hundredweights and tons. It didn't seem to take account of babies. Somewhere she had made a list – a list that was going to change her life and make everything all right. But she'd gone and lost it. It was mostly shopping. She had planned to order a lot of toys from expensive shops: then great packing cases would arrive and the children would take days undoing them. She decided to go to the Cash and Carry – she wouldn't need to find her list because she'd see everything there.

* * *

It was a festival of spending. She and Tim each had a long trolley, Jonny sat on hers holding tins of biscuits and free samples of margarine, then Seth started screaming so he had to have a trolley too. He kept knocking his into the side and bringing down showers of Teddy-bears on pre-Christmas display. Maro was efficient. She piled on sacks of sugar and flour and bright packets of cereals and tins of soup and baked beans. The boys ran ahead filling up their trolleys and picking up the numerous jars that fell off and rolled along the ground.

At the end everything was counted and put into cardboard boxes and Maro made out a cheque for sixty-two pounds. They filled the car, sugar tumbling out of bags, and the baby plunging in fingers.

At home they stored the food round the kitchen and the living-room. She sat and looked at it.

'Now Tim, whenever you're hungry you can walk round and eat whatever you feel like – we won't have any more cooking or plates – just spoons and eat out of tins. We'll pretend we are living on a desert island and the food has to last us for three months.'

Yes, she was getting herself organized – now they were organized they could spend the days playing and being happy . . .

*     *     *

But how did one play and be happy? Yes, she remembered mothers in Mexico – babies in blankets on their backs – and the flooding envy she felt, to feel the warm baby heavy on her back, a fullness – why couldn't she make it that way, what went wrong?

*     *     *

In the hospital Ricci too was getting himself together. The routine he enjoyed, the nurses were beautiful and he had become a star. He was handsome and his thin handsome softness inspired a wonderful pity in the beautiful nurses. When his mother arrived in a broadtail coat with a chauffeur carrying a trough garden he saw Jilly's eyes light up. (Jilly was his favourite nurse.)

'Would you like coffee, Mrs Palmer?' 'Yes please, nurse,' said his mother, and Ricci knew these two women would hit it off, carried into intimacy by their mutual adoration of him, whereas Maro was so remote that his mother loathed her.

And the trough garden, he was slightly embarrassed by it till his mother had left but then he examined it carefully. It stretched the whole length of the window-sill by his bed, thirty inches long and twelve inches wide. It was a somewhat formal layout with a semicircular pool, flanked on either side by a slender juniper, and by the pool a tiny silver Cupid from the top of one of his mother's early Victorian teaspoons.

In the pool floated some tiny plants, microscopic ferns, each little frond with a hair-like root floating upon the water in intricate patterns – he could see his eye-ball reflected in the one corner that wasn't covered in plants.

Maro arrived struggling with a suitcase full of books. She kissed him and sat on the bed but he was half longing for her to leave so he could call Jilly to help him arrange the books and cushions to, as Jilly said, 'make it look like home'. But – although he didn't tell Jilly – it wasn't like home, that continually erupting volcano where nothing was ever in the same place, rather it was his own perfect kingdom suspended still under the sea, the octopus's garden in the shade – below the storm.

He had been moved into a private room with french windows out on to the veranda where, when it was sunny, other patients sat out in wheel-chairs, well wrapped in rugs.

Maro left, leaving the books in piles on the table beside his bed. Among the Dostoievsky and volumes of modern poetry he found what he was looking for: *Multiple Sclerosis: Case Histories*. Fuller and Lowe. He wanted to learn all about his disease, now, while he still had the energy to confront his position; if he could do this quickly before he had fully realized what had happened to him he knew he would be in a stronger position – the alternative was to put his life in other people's hands but first he must see the possibilities. He had a strange sensation that his hour of liberation had come. It was true that nearly all sensation, except vague pins and needles, had left his legs and yet his brain, his head, felt lip up, on fire, a dense tropical garden untouched by human feet – wild country – dangerous country, and yet at last he could feel the strength filling his nerve-endings, the strength to explore, to say goodbye to endless interruptions of ordinary life – being a lawyer, a dad, a rich man's son – and enter a wider country totally his own. He opened the thick book somewhere in the middle and read:

> Case 18. An unmarried female aged 34 was admitted on January 13th, 1964, with a history of an acute retrobulbar neuritis in November 1963. In October 1964 she again complained of mistiness of vision, and also of weakness of the legs and unsteadiness in walking. Ten days before admission paraplegia had advanced rapidly and she had become apathetic. Physical examination on admission to hospital confirmed the diagnosis of multiple sclerosis. C.S.F. 18 cells per c. mm., protein 45 mg. per 100 m.l. Langë colloidal gold curve, strongly paretic. A week later she became confused and doubly incontinent. On February 13th an E.E.G. was quite abnormal without localizing features. An air encephalogram showed a moderate degree of

symmetrical ventricular dilation. Further deterioration occurred so that five weeks later she lay in bed whining noisily, incapable of recognizable speech, refusing to obey commands and, at times, striking those who attended her with the left arm (the only limb in which power remained).

She died in a mental hospital on March 31st, one year and four months after the onset of her illness.

'Wow,' thought Ricci. He bent over his garden and saw a tiny ivy-leafed campanula with slender trailing stems and pale green leaves wind among the damp moss near the pond.

* * *

Outside, the sky was unbroken grey. It rained a little, bursting in tiny blasts against the window-panes. Inside it was warm. She could hear the children quarrelling downstairs as they helped themselves to Weetabix.

What would she do today – there was no school, it was near Christmas. She thought she'd have a bath – that would pass an hour or so.

Lately I have been smelling different – no longer sweet but sour – a sour sweat hangs about me – I notice it in bed at night – once the bed smelt of love and now it smells sad and I no longer like the smell of my own body.

She read somewhere that incidents of multiple sclerosis were very rare in hot countries. So it was to do with the sun. Yes, the body and physical pleasures were to her wedded by the sun. How little real physical pleasure could be had without the sun? Almost none. Flesh had to be warmed by the sun to come alive – it pined away without it and so the nerves became bare and anguished.

What can I do today – the rain shatters me. I'll make bread – the children will help me.

It was difficult to get at the sack of flour, it was underneath so many other things. Eventually she left it to Tim who made a hole somewhere in the middle of it with his penknife and scooped it out with his hands – a lot of it fell on the carpet, but never mind. She read the instructions carefully and Tim, who was ten, helped her, He was her favourite really – he was the most like her, locked away in a dream world, not demanding contact, hardly speaking.

It was Seth who exhausted her most. Jonny she could usually trick into thinking they had made contact with some kisses and sweeties and her purse to tidy but it was Seth who drove her to madness – his father's favourite – who persistently asked for his father and appeared to miss him more than the others. A small boy of five – particularly sensitive and soft, who dreamt a lot and had a wild mind. Also this child couldn't bear her being angry with him – it drove him to untold screaming misery, where even in her desperation and his desperation they couldn't get close to one another – they couldn't somehow make it together and when in the end she would cry, he would cry louder and look into her face, his red wet face, mouth open howling begging, and she empty, empty inside had nothing, nothing to offer his screaming heart; the only thing she could do was to scream too, and then they fell asleep in one another's arms.

In the night he was crying and Maro went to him. 'I had a bad dream,' he said. His face was white and eyes dark in the glow of the night-light. 'I dreamt you didn't like me any more.'

She bent her head. 'Move over and I'll sit beside you.' He wriggled over to the side of the bed, she sat beside him and held his hand. He went on sucking his empty bottle, looking into her eyes and holding her hand. After a while he said, 'You can go now.'

She tried to think what her life consisted of; it seemed to be of walking from one room to another in great disorder and continual forgetfulness, of never having anything she wanted to hand – a sea of disorder, toys, clothes, books, letters.

Last night I dreamt I had cancer and I was overjoyed. Picking the threads off the carpet and my life trickling by. Involved and fascinated by picking the threads off the carpet, the tiny thread, yellow, curling. I spot it, stalk it, trap it. I have it. Caught in my hand and into the wastepaper-basket you go, gold thread, but it clings, the gold thread clings to my hand, it doesn't want to go into the basket. It stays curled on my hand, hanging on, it wants to live in comfort, not the bleak wind of council dumps.

Today I am going to try – I am going to wear a dress and make bread and wash the kitchen floor and be a perfect mother.

She was coring cooking-apples to go with the fish fingers, some delicious recipe, stuffed with dates. She stuck the sharp knife into the apple and turned – the knife flew at her finger and bit into flesh. She saw the great open flap of flesh hanging heavy and white and bloodless for a moment and then the blood poured out and a leaping ache shot through her. She wanted to scream at some man for help. Why wasn't Ricci here when she'd cut her finger?

Tim came in. 'Mum, you're bleeding. Why did you cut yourself? I'll get the plasters. Poor Mum. Why are you wearing a skirt, I like you better in trousers.' Seth came in and galloped round the room halloaing, his high voice piercing her brain like shrapnel.

She took Jonny in her arms and tried to suck some nourishment from his body. She put her face against his belly and breathed in his warmth while her blood dripped on to her bare legs.

*      *      *

What Maro felt was really terror. Terror of the night and day, terror of life and all its horror – how could she bear the sheer terror of the night? Terror when she saw the lamb stew – see how easily the meat falls off the bone – the voice of pleasure which he said it in – look how easily the meat falls off the bone. Rotting flesh filled her with horror. Terror even of real entanglement with her children – that they would ask of her that which she hadn't got.

In the night and I can't sleep and my anxiety seems the only real state to be in, if he dies I won't let them take his body away; I'll bury it here with me, I'll hang on to it. I won't let them take his body. I'll bury him at night in the garden and go on telling the neighbours he's alive, they'll never know, that old piece of stone I found under a pile of rubbish with a carved gothic pattern on it, that'll do as a grave-stone. I'll carve his name myself, just his name. Can I do it myself or will I hurt my fingers with the chisel?

But how can I stand his dying – the abundance of grief, I can't stand it. I will just scream and scream and scream and hold him till he rots to death in my arms and the meat falls off his bones.

Jonny is leaning towards me, his mouth wide open for kissing – he kisses me, his mouth stretches open, his shiny white teeth, his tongue stuck out, he presses his cool open mouth against mine and wriggles his small warm tongue. I carry him on my hip, he uses me like a horse, kicking me this way and that to show him whatever he may want to see and bending backwards rigid and screaming if I don't obey his commands.

'This,' he shouts and I go towards it because if I don't the screams begin.

Then all three are crying, the cries go right through her and seem to tear her to pieces, shred by shred, long red sinews, tendrils of her body torn out to fly like flags of destruction, decimated, stretched apart like a Christian martyr on the rack, like Jayne Mansfield's hair after she was decapitated, like the scream of Munch.

* * *

Last night she dreamt her womb dropped out as she was getting on a bus.

She filled the bath up and got in – to get away from them – but she could still hear them fighting and calling her so she put her head under the water to dim the noise. She could still hear them and yet the sound came from another world and troubled her less – her hair spread out around her on the surface of the water and for a moment she felt alone, a glorious aloneness – in her own world, cut off, free, alone, and then she felt small fingers scrabbling at her hair, winding strands and pulling and the small demanding voice chiming in her ears, dragging out of her some response and the constant chatter of Seth asking his ever more deep and complicated questions, so she felt his mind growing as her own diminished.

And all the time this immense pressure on her chest weighing her down, squashing her so that she could only breathe in quick little pants like a dog that has got too hot by the fire – a throbbing misery – an eternal beating down on some raw place. Then Seth and Jonny came into the bath after her, delighted once more to be in contact with her body, lying on her stomach, both competing for the comfiest place on her body.

They are a flock of wild birds settling in her hair, exploding in her ears and her eyes, a buzz of bees, swarming, clutching round her heart so she cannot see anything except their faces, their limbs, and hear the sound of their voices and she constantly repeating over to herself their names like some magic song over and over. Slowly she went stiller and stiller till she became quiet, still, and they in their franticness not to lose her, buzzed louder after her.

She allowed the children to destroy all those objects she had so carefully got together – slowly she allowed them to be torn to pieces around her – she played the gramophone and lay on the bed, the great raft. In the night the violent dreams, acts of violence tearing her to pieces, the headaches – she would wake up trembling.

Having meant you couldn't be good – because if you were good you'd give it away, and then you wouldn't have it, so you didn't give it away, you didn't really feel you could manage without it – a house and making it warm and buying toys for the children who wanted toys.

Tim, Tim, Tim, Tim. She said her son's name over to herself again and again. Who is Tim? How can she join the little boy she knew to this name? She began to feel dizzy, the name merged for a moment with the boy and then disappeared again. This is my son, look at his smile, he smiles, his teeth. I must take him to the dentist. How can I get to the dentist, he won't want to go?

It was so dark – eleven o'clock in the morning and December outside the window; a moth-eaten tree, still hung about with green and gold leaves, quivered in the cold windless morning.

It was so quiet, just the sound of water running up and down the pipes. She didn't know why, she didn't understand it, the central heating system. She couldn't understand it, the tappets and the time clock and the hot water tank. How did the hot water get from the boiler to the bathroom upstairs, how did water run uphill? What if on a hot day all the water in the world started running uphill?

But that wasn't happening. It was quiet. Opposite in Richmond Park a man was walking with his dog, wrapped up, busy keeping warm. But they'd had this double glazing put in – it had been Ricci's idea – so they wouldn't hear any traffic. He said, 'We live here, so there's no point in sparing any expense in the house you live in.' Yet it was a prison because you heard no noise except the noise you made yourself echoed back to you. You couldn't hear the man's feet crunching on the wet sticks and hear what he called to his dog. You could only see his mouth open and a faint cloud of steam pour into the icy air.

Imprisoned in this house she must get out. She must see someone, touch someone, taste the spit from someone else's mouth and smell their warm unique smell, know, recognize their smell. All these strangers walking past wrapped against the weather. She remembered bare limbs in the summer, bare legs touching beneath her cotton dress. So why wear clothes if the house is so warm, it's too hot to wear clothes. She took off the children's clothes and watched them playing naked, rolling over one another, and Jonny just standing peeing on the carpet and smiling at her over his shoulder. She looks at them, she is imprisoned by Jonny banging the tin tray on the wooden floor – how many different sounds he can make with it.

Why can't they be three naked men, footballers perhaps,

the cool winter, winter afternoon, their hot bodies one after another to take her and love her, and another and another till she'd had all of them, even the beefy red-faced goalie with the thick black hair sticking up porcupine-fashion over his big face.

The desire came over her to escape, to run away – just to leave everything and walk out, to be alone away, just herself.

Seth climbed on to her knees and battened her down with his love, kissed her face and insisted on sucking her nose and pushing her backwards in the chair, little arms around her neck, crooning, 'No, no, you can't get up, stay there!' and soon the baby had joined him and shrieked to be allowed up too and she had lifted him up on to her lap and felt completely swamped, wiped out, no longer existing under the two vigorous bodies, the energy flying out of every part of them, their faces, mouths, hands, and scrabbling feet pushing her backwards till she was completely powerless, imprisoned by their vibrant spirits. Small, vigorous limbs and wet mouths chanting weird chants breaking into laughter, shouts or cries, the never-ending demanding cries of such small people. Those small legs and hard wriggling bodies and flailing hands and sweet dribble, eating me up. My mind, my ears, my eyes constantly tuned to your safety, my anxiety drawn, stretched around you, never to feel my own passion. I can think only of you and want to touch your small perfect limbs. They scream, they demand, but devious, sly and cold they never are. They never calculate or plot against you, or long for your ruin. Childlike love – it is hard to resist and yet within her she felt a tiny core of resistance, a hard pellet of gunpowder which could explode.

*   *   *

Once when Maro was fifteen her sister had a party. Lots of young men in black with shiny shoes. Maro found them all stunning and did not know which to fall in love with.

It was her sister's idea – 'You must dance your Dance of the Seven Veils, Maro, naked underneath and all my coloured scarves waving around you.'

'I wouldn't dare.'

'Drink this gin, I'll tell no one, then when I put your special record on I'll clap my hands, tell everyone to stand back and you appear.'

Maro drank the gin – the party was a great success, the music, voices, laughter. She waited shivering naked in the next room. She heard her sister clapping her hands – she heard her record. High on a windy hill – she came in to a crowd of faces. She began to dance – she heard her sister's excited giggle. She felt the floor hard beneath her bare feet. She leapt and spun and flung off her veils – each inch of her body was vibrating – her tangled hair flew around her face – her mouth was open. She felt a queen – a princess – a king.

The record stopped and she opened her arms as though to embrace her audience. She felt so open, open, full of love.

And then she noticed the faces – a kind of horror. Her sister was clapping and smiling and saying 'Hurrah'. But next to her the blond young man – her favourite – the most handsome and dashing – stood stiff, waves of shock smoking from his body, his face frozen with disgust ...

Ricci now had a collection of tools laid out on a silk scarf in the corner of the window-sill. A tiny enamel watering-can with a very fine rose – so fine that even dust in the water clogged up the holes – every day he had to take it off and clean it by submerging it in a bowl of boiling water brought to him by Jilly. She had also given him a book called *Gardens on a Higher Level* which was all about trough gardens and how to care for them. His mother had sent a cut-glass perfume spray with a silver top; this he used for damping the tiny leaves throughout the day when the heat from the radiator made them look dry. From Jilly he had got a pair of eyebrow tweezers for pulling up the smallest weeds. He had asked Maro to bring him an old fork for digging and hoeing. She had brought him a silver one with a green jade handle; it was from a canteen of fish knives and forks they had been given as a wedding present and never used. Typical of Maro to disregard the value – still, he enjoyed using the fork with the delicate Victorian tracery.

Then there was a paint-brush for removing soil and dust from low-growing plants. And finally a magnifying glass for identifying insect pests, because it said in his book, 'Insect pests if left unchecked can do a great deal of damage.'

So Ricci spent a good deal of time with his magnifying

glass, carefully lifting the delicate leaves of plants in search of the devastating red spider mite

> not easily recognized because it hides under the surface of the leaves of roses and primulas and in-between the tiny needles of conifers and it is so minute ... Hardly visible to the naked eye, the effect of their presence can be deduced from the mottled yellowish patches of the foliage. If this is examined under a magnifying glass, the pests can be seen. However, it is easy to be misled, as they are not really spiders and only red at one stage of their lives, more often green with microscopic black marks on their backs. Sometimes one can see only their eggs. Red spider mites usually remain almost stationary, sucking the sap from the foliage. They should not be confused with a beautiful coral-red velvety spider which is a friendly insect and moves quickly in or on the soil ...

So Ricci leant over his garden, his glass to his eye, hoping to see a friendly spider – the space beneath the plants seemed enormous and each day something changed. Plants and insects were rewarding to love – unlike people and animals they left the nerves intact and the senses unshattered.

His involvement with Jilly grew too. He found her physically comforting – the way the buttons on her uniform sometimes popped open around her breasts when she lifted him up and the way she didn't seem to mind if her hair came down and tumbled over one shoulder as she said, holding the sponge, 'Are you going to wash Percy – which was the name she had given his penis – or am I?'

And when he was gloomy and just lay there not even bothering with his garden, she would come briskly in – 'my working walk' she called it – and say, 'What's all the fuss about – take it easy – everything's so simple really.' She was so much more present than Maro. The elusive Maro.

He didn't love Jilly – he was sure of that and yet ... how come she wanted so little out of life? How come she liked washing his body? And she must like it because of the way she did it and the time she took over it – often she'd stop in the middle and point out to him a bird on the lawn – she knew all the different bird names and noticed the variations in their feathers as she noticed his body – a tiny birth-mark below his left nipple and the way hairs grew up his back-bone. It was through her he learnt to look at things really closely: to see on moonlit nights the grass curl against the cold, and the minute variations in his own body, his skin and sensations going on inside his muscles, his pain, his release from pain as he takes the drug and in a curious way his addiction to his pain, his addiction to his awareness, having the time to be aware each moment of just what is happening to him. The very first sensation of wanting to pee and the feeling of relief afterwards, the incredible tuning-in to his sick body. Sometimes after he had eaten, the colly-wobbles came – it perfectly described the fluttering sickness in his guts.

But with Jilly behind him he felt courageous and heard himself saying to the consultant, 'All I ask is that you tell me the whole truth. Don't distance me from my true situation; by doing that you isolate me from myself and the real world – that is what makes me intolerably lonely. Tell me everything.' The consultant was impressed.

That night Ricci wrote in his journal:

Today my Cornish moneywort flowered – so tiny that they can only be seen by the magnifying glass, creamy white against their pale green foliage. Mr Rickshaw examined me. I told him I wanted only the truth. In a minute Jilly will bring me my Ovaltine before she goes home. It is the smell I like even better than the taste. Another full and happy day has passed.

It was Christmas Eve – Richmond Park was white, it had snowed in the night. The trees were frozen. Maro dressed the children up warm, Jonny in a red siren suit that zipped right up and a white Balaclava with a peak, his tiny face almost hidden except for two large brown eyes and a small nose.

They went down across the common to where the undergrowth is thick and wild. Tim ran on ahead climbing trees and jumping down, helping Seth, who was a bit of a coward, up a few feet till he shouted to get down and rushed to his mother's side.

It is a perfect day, brother sun shines – the sky completely blue. Time standing still, suspended.

'Where is your mind?' asks Seth. 'If you cut somebody up all over would you find their mind?'

Tim brings a twig with brown leaves turned to ice. He licks it. Jonny yells for it and he gives it to him to eat.

'I know what love is,' says Seth. 'First you find someone and you think they look nice, then you run away with them and then when you get to know them you fall in love with them.'

The wind blew, forcing the sludge out of my eyes. Jonny rode on my hip kicking me if I didn't keep up with Tim and Seth, shouting at me to lift him on to branches of trees. We found a sheltered spot and sat in the snow huddled together and ate some chocolate, the sun on our faces.

Tim and Seth both peed to see who could melt the most snow and then Jonny wanted to as well which was an awful business as he had his siren suit and a nappy on, but we managed. 'Do men have longer pee-pees so that they don't have to go pee-pee so often?' asked Seth.

How strange I feel happy, so extraordinarily happy. There are two blackbirds quite still on a branch. Does money make happiness? Once I asked a woman, 'Did your Mum have a garden, May?' 'No, she never had the money for seeds.'

Tim was making a collection of objects – a fir cone, a lemonade bottle, a red plastic shuttlecock; he arranged them all in a pile of snow at their feet. 'When ladies go swimming why do they wear bosom bras?' asked Seth.

'It's silly really,' said Maro. 'It feels so much nicer without. When I was a girl, Aunty Jane and I swam naked in the river when no one was around. It was lovely the cool water on my body.' God, how alive she had felt, each nerve, each blood-vessel, as they had leapt and laughed naked in the icy river water.

Jonny climbed on to my knees and rubbed his cold face and his wet mouth against mine, his hard white teeth banging up against my face. His warm wet gravy-smelling breath. Seth, laughing, climbed on to my legs, putting his arms around Jonny and kissing my face, then Tim came up. 'I'm the most important,' and tried to climb on too. So I fell backwards in the snow and the three little boys tumbled over my chest and head and arms, their sweet bodies weighing me down deep into the cold snow – their warm hands on my face, their voices in my ears – till I felt totally dissolved, borne away on the sweetness of their laughter.

It began to snow, enormous white flakes. If only it could cover us quickly and we could sleep and play beneath the pure white blanket.

Maro is sitting in a glass room. One side looks out on to a carpeted corridor up and down which people purposefully hurry with papers clutched in their hands or under their arms. The three other sides look into other rooms where people sit at desks with typewriters, and busy themselves tap-tap tapping out some Morse code.

There is a shiny table in the glass room round which she and two dark-suited gentlemen sit. One of these is the accountant and the other the family financial adviser who is young and handsome and calls her familiarly by her first name.

'What have you spent – ten and a half thousand pounds on, Maro?'

'I don't know,' she said.

'You appear to live so simply – you have no help in the house – you say your neighbour takes the children in when you visit the hospital. Do you pay *her* anything?'

'No, she likes having them, she's always tempting them through the fence with bananas and titbits – she has no children of her own – "Go on holiday, Maro," she says, "I'll have the children, go round the world if you like." … Perhaps I should, Robert?' She felt her mind go blank as she looked at him. She saw his face and his eyes smiling friendlily at her. He had full lips slightly parted – child's lips. What was he like at home?

'Do you realize that's two hundred pounds a week you've been spending?' said Robert.

'Two hundred pounds a week,' she thought, 'that doesn't sound very much – how can I manage on two hundred pounds a week?' She had a sensation of weightlessness, of floating and everything floating around her. She felt a moment of total panic – these men were telling her she had spent far too much money – she would have to cut down drastically – yet how could she possibly do it?

How could she live on less? She tried to remember what it said in her *Commercial Man's Guide*; she thought it was only about one hundredweight of lead. She just couldn't manage on a hundredweight of lead.

The two men were looking at her – she liked them both. They were turning over a great sheaf of papers that had her name in block letters on its blue folder – perhaps they'd be able to find out how she'd spent the money. She felt a momentary surge of relief and with sudden brightness she said, 'Have you got any children, Mr Bond?'

He looked surprised but smiled and said, 'Yes, I've two small girls.'

'Well, I expect they get at you to buy them lots of dolls and pretty dresses.' She remembered a woman at a party, capable, open-eyed – I must pretend to be her – She rattled on brightly ... 'The cost of things these days – by the time I've bought the groceries, and the boys wear their clothes out so quickly, and then there's the soap powder I get through. I've tried working out which is the most economical – Daz or Tide or Omo – but they all seem to be expensive ... ' If only she could make them love her like they loved their wives everything would be all right.

'… And then there's Jonny. He will keep getting into my purse and tearing up notes. Perhaps that's how I get through so much,' and Maro's face broke into a smile as she thought she may have found the answer. But kind Mr Bond's face only showed startled amazement and Robert's a shocked concern.

'So you let him tear up notes?'

'Well sometimes I just can't stop him – you see, he likes to tidy my bag.'

She lifted her great heavy shoulder bag off the floor and put it on her knees and unzipped it. 'He might have hidden some in here.' She put in her hand, the bag was full of bits of paper and pennies and silver coins – she hadn't realized there was so much in there. No wonder it was so heavy and cut deep into her shoulder when she walked.

'Would you mind if I turned it out on the table?'

'No, go ahead, go ahead,' said Robert.

Out poured a jumble of pennies, shillings, screwed-up pound notes, a little sheaf of neatly tied ten-pound notes, a hairbrush, and a book of poetry.

She began to count it and put it into little piles.

'I think I spend rather a lot on bath essence, but there again it's Jonny's fault, he keeps knocking the bottles into the bath and they smash and tiny pieces of sharp glass lie in an orange puddle – so I have to scoop it up in my flannel and throw the whole flannel away and then buy a new one, and by the time I've bought more bath essence – and sometimes I don't know which to choose and have to take two or three bottles – that must account for a pound or two.'

'It must be expensive bath essence you go in for,' said Robert drily.

'Yes, well that's why I bought this notebook. I wanted to work out about bulk buying – I thought if I went in for bulk buying and stocked up well in advance it would leave me free for living.'

'For living?' Robert asked.

'Yes, when I see something I like, it seems a waste of time thinking about whether I should buy it or not, better to buy it, take it home and see – it will probably come in handy and if not I can always give it away.'

She saw Robert looking at her quite tenderly.

'If I was married to you,' she said, 'I expect I'd be all right – you'd tell me what to do and how to manage, wouldn't you?'

She looked at his hands and thought they were nice. She looked at his eyes – what were they doing in this office? 'When I went to the hospital yesterday there was this postcard stuck up by the receptionist's office. It was Connemara I think – a soft green hill and a lake and long grass and a misty sun. It would be nice to go there together and get to know one another better.'

She saw Robert struggling to keep his man-of-the-world smile – Mr Bond laughed indulgently and shut up his papers and looked at his watch.

'I expect he's thinking about his little girls and their beautiful little arms and legs.'

Maro's head was bursting with trying to remember what she was meant to be doing with Robert and Mr Bond in the strange room. Was it a honeymoon in Ireland they were there to organize – because love was all there was really, when it came to it.

Mr Bond put the thick elastic band round the folder and looked at his watch again.

'Well, I'll do all I can for you, Mrs Palmer. I'll work out some system so you only spend a certain amount each week.'

Maro jumped to her feet and caught hold of Mr Bond's

warm hand. 'Thank you so much, Mr Bond – I know I'll be all right if you do that – if I can leave absolutely everything to you I know I won't go wrong.'

'Well, I'll say goodbye then.'

When Mr Bond had gone Robert said to her, 'You could be a beautiful woman, Maro, if you bought yourself some nice clothes – if you're going to spend all that money you might at least dress well.'

'I'd like to,' said Maro, 'in fact I thought I was well dressed.' She looked down at her body. 'Don't you like this jumper?'

It was an old green Shetland one her father had given her. Now it was shrunk and one of the sleeves was frayed, but it was a beautiful colour and over it she wore a leather-thonged waistcoat. 'This waistcoat is the latest thing out, Robert,' she said.

'I'd love to see you in a beautiful dress,' he said.

She wondered if he really cared about her – if he'd run away with her and look after her.

'Love is all there is,' she said.

He looked totally disarmed now. 'Yes' – he saw her out of the office – 'I suppose you're right. Love is all there is.'

* * *

Maro walked off through the city along crowded pavements in the direction of home.

So what about this money business? She tried to remember the really best things in her life and how much they had cost. Swimming in that river in Scotland and seeing her body gold and naked under the water – swimming up towards the waterfall and turning round and drifting, gliding down with the current, the cold water between her legs and on her face and eyes, and dipping her head under – under – Then climbing on to the bank and shaking the water off her naked body – she had no towel – and lying on the rough turf and drying in the sun.

But could she really fling off the oppressors or did she need them? Did she need them to clothe and feed her, to tell her that she was clever and remind her what her name was?

For a moment she couldn't even remember if she was a man or a woman.

Once upon a time she had understood about money but now it had turned into a code she couldn't break. She couldn't master it, the harder she tried the less sense it made – '£5 for 5 minutes of lovely lust with Gay', she read on a notice board and next to it, 'Legless man, NOT invalid, requires housekeeper, could pay £3 a week plus own room.'

In a butcher's shop-window, hung about with the hairless bodies of dead animals, a large placard said 'Sausages 3/6 a pound.' But her canary had only cost twelve and six and her canary sang – perhaps the sausages sang too and she'd never noticed.

And so it struck her as a mad complicated code without reason and yet understood and clung to with such violence by everyone else that when she gave the woman the wrong money for some hangers in Woolworth's, she took it as some personal affront. Maro rushed out into the air, feeling she was going to cry, that woman was so angry with her – I would have liked to give her double, but then Robert would be at me.

Everything bruised her, the man on the tube looked sad, looked dirty – he couldn't catch hold of the tassel. He stumbled, he had a scar on his lip and an old pair of shoes. Perhaps he hadn't got any money. Should she give him some?

She unzipped her bag and put her hand into the pile of coins, but then he might be angry with her or think she was a prostitute and want to fuck her. That had happened once to a friend of hers late at night between Stratford East and Bow. They had been the only two in the carriage and he had fucked her between stations and then hopped out when the train stopped before she could ask him his name. Shortly afterwards the girl had killed herself – Maro knew it was because it had all got out of hand – and so she zipped up her bag again because nowhere in her memory could she find a reference to dirty men on tube trains and if you were allowed to give them money.

She got off the train. She felt better now she was in the suburbs. There weren't so many people about to see her if she did freak out.

The sky is mottled with iron-grey clouds. The pond water is almost black – two boys send a clockwork tug over its dark surface. The grass is dark green, the trees are massive and black.

She remembered the summer. Dr Scholl's sandals and bare legs and posies of little girls with prams and cotton dresses on the pavement and boys with tricycles at their garden gates and pigeons under the bridge and a faint breeze and sparrows singing a suburban song and people enjoying their gardens. And her own garden, the trellis of honeysuckle in the early morning. And my children talk to me – chitter chatter like starlings on a roof top. My children. My Tim wanting me, silent, difficult, my Seth, my little chatterbox, my star, my Jonny, small, impenetrable – without them I would rather not be alive. My little loves, it is you I need and love above any man. The mad busy world can't touch us as long as we have lots of money. The world goes mad – people bully each other, hate each other, make each other shed hot running tears that drop off cheeks, huge tear-drops squeezed out of sad hearts.

Maro came to her own house. In the summer the lime trees and the horse-chestnut full of sunlight dappling the kitchen floor and falling into the stainless steel sink. And this pavement with the uneven shady brickwork down the centre.

As she opened the gate Seth ran to meet her. He held up his small white arm. 'I hurted and bruisded myself,' he said.

She saw the streak of blood and the grazed flesh on his thin white arm, and thought, 'How can I protect him?'

Soaking up the warmth from the flannel sheets – stay here, don't move, don't feel – don't speak and you will be all right – I wanted it to be just me and my children perfect love. She made a list of things she needed to go out into the world – one rabbit-skin coat with a hood and a red flannel lining, one pair of boots, one pair of jeans, and no feelings.

She went to the hospital. By this time Ricci's room was full of tiny troughs, pottery seed pans and packets of John Innes Compost No. 2.

'Look Maro,' said Ricci, as Maro, long hair wet from the drizzle, came in. 'Look at this pan of rose-cuttings, see, already they have taken and are rising up on their buoyant little roots demanding to be potted. When Jilly gets here we'll pot them.'

Maro bent over the tiny plants and saw their perfect minute leaves and yet somehow she couldn't connect. She couldn't see what these dear little plants had to do with her own life.

Jilly came in. 'Hello,' she said. 'Isn't it a horrid day?'

Maro, who hadn't noticed the weather, raced desperately round her memory and looked out of the window at the slaty sky. 'Yes,' she said to Jilly, who was by this time bending over one of the troughs, the cloth of her uniform tight across her buttocks.

'How do you keep warm in those thin clothes?' asked Maro, who herself had a bright red jumper and an Afghanistan waistcoat and brown trousers.

'Good circulation I suppose,' said Jilly, rubbing her smooth skin.

'Don't you think they're ready for potting, Jilly?' said Ricci.

'I think it's because you're busy and healthy,' said Maro thoughtfully.

'You must be even busier with those three little boys,' said Jilly.

'Oh yes,' said Maro surprised. 'I suppose I must.'

There was so much rubbish to clear away. She filled boxes with rubbish but the dust-man wouldn't take it and it remained, a great sordid pile around the front gate, stray pieces of butter paper sticking like flags to the wooden gate-posts. But this wasn't exactly busy – or was it? She didn't feel she had a full rich life and yet somehow Jilly did.

She and Ricci were examining the cuttings together. 'See this one, he hasn't come on at all.' So roses even had sexes – there was so much she didn't know about gardening. Maro wished she knew a lot about everything. 'People who know a lot are never at a loss,' she had once read somewhere. She thought it was in *Mother's World*.

'I think I'll go and help with lunches,' said Maro, who by now was quite well known at the hospital and wandered about helping nurses with various chores.

She had begun to do this after arriving one day and finding Ricci so involved in his own blissful silence that he didn't really even want her in the room – and yet she liked coming, and anyway people seemed to expect her to come.

First she fed Miss Starkey. Old and fragile, eating her

dinner in her wheel-chair, her grey hair falling over her face almost touching the gravy. The brown fur tippet round her shoulders – soft shiny fur – her glass eyes and the permanent smile on her small face, as Maro put spoonfuls of mince and hot mash into her mouth.

And later undressing her for her afternoon sleep, her cold swollen feet; kneeling on the floor in front of her, warming her cracked feet in her hands before putting on her blue angora bed socks. Miss Starkey smiling as we carry her into bed, her skin, her bones, old lady, bone-thin legs and cold feet tucked in, her bed shawl round her shoulders, ear-phones lying by her side in case she should like to hear the crackling tones of afternoon music.

As Maro was there Nurse Hastings asked her to help with a couple of 'lifts'. First they did Mrs Carr, with one side of her face paralysed. She carried on doing her knitting and talking of her daughter till nurse said, 'You're not concentrating, Mrs Carr.'

Then there was Mrs Church, the legless Mrs Church – like a side of lamb hanging in the butcher's Christmas window. Her bewildered face and constant cries to God, and her smell. 'Help, help,' she would shout and sometimes she would be given a Disprin to help.

Miss Edwin was Maro's favourite. Maro always fed her last because she never seemed to be hungry. Also, she had lost her sense of taste and so eating was no great thrill for her.

She had wide-open pale blue eyes like sea pearls, washed over and over with tears till the colour had almost gone – sea pebbles from the deep.

Maro was told she hadn't spoken for five years, although as far as anybody knew she could speak and indeed had spoken on arrival. She had long-fingered hands from the bottom of the ocean. Diving Dolly she was known as, from her young days when she was a well-known figure on the board.

Maro fed her milk pudding with a dollop of raspberry jam on top, mixing it round so it swirled into pink, remembering the ice-cream man, the green summer evening street – asking me what flavour ice I wanted, nut chocolate or raspberry nipple – he was Maltese, he must have meant 'ripple'.

And Miss Edwin, who was having lunch in bed today because she'd had a slight stroke two days before, stretched out her hand to Maro and Maro held it as she fed her. Maro smiled but Miss Edwin just stared at her, a penetrating gone, high kind of stare, not offensive but just as if she was looking at someone she liked and yet an earth creature whereas she herself was – flown away. No shame, no physical anchors, a bareness, a total openness – see me, this wasted body, I hold your hand.

Beside the bed was Miss Edwin's canvas wheel-chair totally empty except for two cushions Maro had brought her. When Maro gave them to her Miss Edwin lifted each elbow in turn for Maro to put them under. This was her only acknowledgment of the gift. Most of the other ladies had their wheel-chairs stuffed with belongings – boxes of Kleenex, purses, knitting, combs, library books, letters, photographs, sweets. Miss Edwin had nothing and appeared totally unconcerned about acquiring anything.

Miss Edwin, Maro felt, was concerned with only one thing and that was the mystery of existence and what she was doing here, semi-paralysed, without taste or physical sensation and yet alive. What could it mean? And so Maro read on her fine face a permanent bewilderment over what it was all about, and so Maro held her hand and sat by her bed and found, Yes, I could easily adapt myself to this hospital life, the hours slip by in a peaceful routine, the nurses, their clean arms and certainty and busy walking on winged feet.

Brown saliva trickled down Miss Edwin's chin on to her flowered bib and Maro wiped her mouth.

When Maro came out into the corridor there was a traffic jam by the sweet shop.

'Oh, buck up, they'll drive me potty,' said Mrs Ray. Mrs Ray had a little electric chair like a palace. It went purring along the passages, flying past the slow coaches. Now she was stuck in the queue and her frustration was mounting. 'Move on, Mrs Crawley, so I can get by you ...'

'My husband always said I only went to the flower-show to look at the men and never to look at the flowers,' she said to Maro. 'Did you know I was very beautiful?'

Maro remembered combing her hair for her and how she had to have it just right and Mrs Ray staring at her crooked face in the mirror. Her small bit of sprouting hair and her thin legs, but her feet are large and swollen and dark blue, with squashed toes like prunes – perhaps not exactly beautiful but unique – unique, certainly.

Ricci had been moved to a hospital outside London to have steroid therapy. Adrenocorticotrophic hormone was the name of the drug injected intra-muscularly every day. Within a fortnight there should be a marked improvement – he might even walk – alternatively he might stay just the same.

Maro was advised not to visit him often, as he was in a special group of four men in a ward and the dosage was experimental.

Jilly was looking after the trough garden and on her days off Maro was going in to do it.

It was strange coming here now Ricci was away. Everybody greeted her, she felt at home, much more than in her own house.

She sprayed the tiny garden with the fine rose and dusted the window-sill.

In the passage she met Miss Brown. 'Oh-you-do-get-about-Mrs-Palmer,' she said haltingly, opening her mouth so wide I can see her tonsils and her black and missing teeth.

'Where are you going, Miss Brown?' 'The ver-an-da.'
'I'll take you there.'

Maro pushed Miss Brown down the corridor. On her way she passed one old lady pushing another old lady in front of her. They were both in wheel-chairs but the one in front had lost the use of her arms.

It was early spring, the sun was out. She sat for a moment on the veranda near Miss Brown, watching the starlings run over the short damp grass to where someone had thrown some crumbs.

Miss Brown had been a cripple all her life. When she was three her father died. 'My mother and I lived in a little house in Carshalton, near the green. In the morning we'd go slowly along to the shops together. In the afternoons, if it was fine, I'd sit out of doors and sew while my mother gardened. We were both mad about music. We had this enormous collection of gramophone records which we'd listen to in the evenings, taking it in turns to choose. One morning my mother didn't come in to get me up. I called her but she never came. I lay in bed for about two days, then a neighbour got in and they found my mother had died, so I came here on my forty-fifth birthday.

'I don't know if I missed anything by not marrying, but I don't think so, we were very happy.' Maro sitting near her felt the happiness of Miss Brown and her mother, those long summer evenings, the windows open to the garden and *La Traviata* on the gramophone ... Why, she and Ricci could – but who would look after the children?

When she got home there was an enormous box from Fortnum and Mason. She opened it; it was a long silver dress, tight, with long tight sleeves like a snake's skin – it was beautiful, but when would she wear it? Ricci didn't usually give her presents except of books to improve her mind. Perhaps he wanted her to wear it when she visited him. It wasn't the kind of dress she ever wore – it was too beautiful, made for some rich pampered darling. But they had told her to expect strange things from Ricci under treatment ... or could it have been

Robert who had sent it? Robert, who if she belonged to him would make her wear beautiful clothes and brush her hair and be proud of her.

They lived totally upstairs now because rats and mice had got into the sacks of flour and sugar she had bought and Jonny had done the rest Like some enemy tank he went slowly through the house leaving a path of destruction – torn paper, clothes pulled off shelves, packets of biscuits broken and strewn across the floor, rolls of lavatory paper unleashed in the bathroom, taps turned on and toys thrown out of the window, and worst of all his bottle lost. His bottle without which he would go nowhere but which he was always losing. So he would begin wailing and she would begin looking, calling them all to help her; sometimes it took as much as an hour and then they'd find one which had been lost weeks before and had green mould growing up its plastic walls. Why did she find it so difficult to make it nice – to have tea in the garden, for the children to run barefoot, for the sun to shine?

But Jonny and Seth were always crying, their little faces distorted and red with cascading wails. Outside the window a silver articulated lorry stopped in the main road; it shone under the budding spring trees. What does it suffer a man if he cannot enter the Kingdom of Heaven. Why can't I enter the Kingdom of Heaven? Bright colours, cool grass and the sun coming out to shine on the silver lorry – I only want to enter the Kingdom of Heaven.

Sometimes I don't care and then other times I feel so sad, so sad I think I'm going to melt. There is a heavy weight across my chest as if part of my body were a corpse. I'm frightened of going to sleep in case I don't wake up.

When she got upstairs Jonny was being sick. Maro picked him up and he clung to her, screaming. Seth was worried. 'He took all the chocolates and I found him eating them behind the curtains.' Seth was beginning to cry too. Tim was lying on the floor in a corner reading a comic – he didn't seem to notice the noise.

Maro tried to put Jonny down so she could comfort Seth and wipe up the sick but he screamed louder and was sick again all over her dress. His face red and ugly and covered with slimy chocolate sick and the smell and his burning cheek burning my cheek, perhaps he's ill, the hot sick baby and his eyes blurred with tears. She carried him into the bathroom and Seth followed crying a little. She filled the basin with water and stood them both on a chair and washed their faces and dried their tears.

'Boats!' shouted Jonny cheerfully.

'Yes, boats! Boats!' shouted Seth imitating him.

She gave them their boats and some clean water, and went to wipe the floor.

Through the open door she looked at her three boys – Tim had now joined them, his hair golden in the sun coming through the window. Jonny was standing perilously on the edge of the lavatory, hands under the tap so drops spurted out over him and the floor, and any minute he would slip and fall and scream and she would have to hold him in her arms and comfort him but where to find the wherewithal to comfort him, better to stop him now before he fell. But he would cry if she stopped him playing with the water and then what would she do with him?

Perhaps the cool spraying water would cool her down. She felt terribly hot – she couldn't understand the central heating, the house was always boiling, in the night she woke up sweating – and now as she looked at the children she had a sense of sliding away, slipping in her own hot sweat.

She decided to wash her hair; that always made her feel better. She bent over the bath and turned on the mixer spray. First it went freezing cold and then boiling hot so it burnt her head – she couldn't believe it wouldn't come the right temperature so she kept her head under the burning water till she was crying with the pain ... Why didn't it come out warm, why was everything becoming more and more difficult to control?

Later that night when the two little ones were at last asleep, she sat with Tim in the dim bedroom. She felt he was trying to approach her in some way, that he wanted to make contact with her. She felt a vague alarm at being asked to be anything except this dispensing machine of food and shelter, but he stayed there and told her about a dream he'd had. He dreamt he was in the Spanish civil war, there were silver aeroplanes full of sun and he was swimming in the sea in his mask and flippers. Slowly she felt herself open and grow soft and still to the whole of him and the still, dim room where they sat on the bed leaning their elbows on the window-sill and looking across the dark common. Open and soft and listening to her son smiling and telling her his dream in his quiet voice, and both of them tired – unusual for them to be up at this late dark hour. She wanted to embrace him, to take him in her arms, to kiss his sweet face like she did the little ones. Tomorrow she would take them all to see their father – Why should she be parted from them even for a split second – weren't they her dear little boys?

'Sleep in here if you like, Timmy,' she said and he climbed into her bed and fell fast asleep. And when, later in the night, Jonny woke her with his cries she carried him and Seth into the bed as well, screwing up every last ounce of energy to comfort the child in the dark night. They lay close by her and when she turned on her side with her back to Seth he poked her till she turned round, and then he said in his small commanding voice, 'Hold my hand.'

Maro managed to get all three boys clean and tidy and on to the train. She wore the long silver dress and her Indian cotton coat.

The hospital had been built as an isolation hospital so it was out in the countryside.

Tim and Seth ran ahead, Tim following the arrows which said 'B wards'. They were spread out: 1930 red-brick bungalow buildings – very different from the beautiful suburban mansion with the cedar trees in the garden, where he had been before.

As they came into the entrance hall he was there waiting for them. He must have seen them coming, through the window. As they came through the glass doors he was still in the corner, sitting in a wheel-chair, but as they came in he pushed himself up on his hands, he stood – he who hadn't stood for two months. There he was standing and then he started walking towards them, stumbling forwards one, two, three steps. Maro put down Jonny and opening her arms ran forward just as Ricci, stumbling a fourth step, collapsed forward on his face. Maro took his weight against her thighs and broke his fall. He lay in the hall as the other visitors hurried by. Maro knelt down, and so did the children, round him – there were no nurses about.

'Are you all right, Ricci?'

'Yes, just help me up.'

Tim and Maro managed to lift him back into the chair. Perhaps there was someone else helping, Maro wasn't clear. She felt sick looking at the sinister wheel-chair, all iron and spikes.

'Will you push me round the out-of-doors?' said Ricci.

They went outside.

He tried to believe it would work, he wanted to give me a surprise, he wanted to be better ... but I thought he liked being ill.

She pushed him slowly along a wooded path towards the cricket field. She bent and picked a wild flower and some hedgerow leaves. The summer had come.

We walked through the grass, he smelt the flowers, the children played in and out of the trees. Over the high fence we saw some pigs rootling in the grass. We went to the café. I have a cup of tea and a soggy sandwich, the children have crisps and sweets. The lady giving out drinks says to the armless child, 'I'm sorry, we've run right out of straws.' She says it with such softness in her voice and Maro listens. She sits on a bench beside Ricci while the children play on the slide and swings. She listens to the talk around her.

'He is cussed and he takes it out on his wife. He won't be helped, he falls and then she has to pick him up and he weighs fifteen stone.'

'How is my garden?' asks Ricci.

'It's fine. Jilly has weeded the pond.'

Jonny runs up, catches her face and spits pink coconut ice into her mouth.

The woman next door continues her story. 'Then he was two months in West Ham plastic surgery hospital, trying to get rid of his bed sores, with a deep infection to the bone, which had to be operated on. In the end he turned his face to the wall and responded to nobody or nothing.'

Maro held Ricci's hand.

'Remember,' he said, 'remember the spring we went to Italy.'

Maro remembered.

'It's all we have really – our memories,' he said.

'No, surely,' she said, 'there must be something else?' But perhaps he was right and in some ways she had never been great shakes on living – just too much experience crowded in on her – Why not just stay with him and smile a little and read books and pretend to live. Surely no one would notice – she was good at acting and used to lying. Yes, that was the answer, she would pretend to live, pretend to be there but really she would abstract herself and live in *War and Peace* and *Anna Karenina* – surely she didn't have to have close relationships or sex for that matter – many people had done very well without it.

The trouble was she didn't really like living. It really was enormously boring to her, the best part of it was just enormously boring, just sometimes when she connected ... but that was so rare she might as well put it out of her mind altogether. She even gave up thinking. She had always cared about thinking, hung on to thought as an important thing in her life, but suddenly she found it no longer mattered to her – she simply ceased to bother.

Yet now as she sat on the grass, Jonny on her lap, and felt the sun seep into her, hot sun in this sheltered place ... the sun brought strength seeping into her bones, opening her heart. Why was she so bad at living?

'Do you mind the dormitory?' she asked Ricci.

'Anything rather than go to bed alone,' he told her. That's why he loved the dormitory and listening to the different breathing, at least he wasn't alone. The air was alive, the coughs and groans of other living creatures thickening the atmosphere. He noticed, when he was on his own, the air became thinner, rarer, he could enter closer to ecstasy and despair.

When he was by himself he became out of control, roaring out into his own madness. Now in the dormitory he was kept on the ground by the endless irritations of his fellow prisoners. He felt at rest in captivity; sometimes at night he could lean out of bed and rest his head on the sill and watch the stars.

The journey home started badly. The taxi turned a corner too sharply and Seth fell off his seat and hurt his head. Maro started to sweat and by the time they got to the station she could feel rivulets of sweat running down her back.

'Twelve and six,' said the driver. Maro looked in her purse. There were many coins in it – in fact as usual it was overflowing from her habit of always paying with notes, even when it was only a shilling, in case she gave the wrong coin. Now it was full of coins and so was the bottom of her bag, but there were no notes.

She picked up a handful.

'How much did you say?'

'Twelve and six,' repeated the driver.

Maro looked carefully at the coins in her hand. Tim was on the pavement holding Seth and Jonny by the hands.

'Twelve and six,' she said out loud as she stared at the coins. The harder she tried to concentrate the more it eluded her. She began to panic – any moment now Jonny would wriggle out of Tim's grasp and career off with his ungainly gait down the pavement. The driver was revving his engine.

She picked two of the brightest coins out of her hand and, with a dazzling smile full of hope, handed them over.

'What's this, then?' said the driver holding the two half-crowns in his hand.

'Your money ... '

'I said "Twelve shillings and sixpence", and anyway these things are long out-of-date.'

'I'll count it, Mum,' said Tim. She opened her hand and slowly and carefully he counted it out, handing it bit by bit to the driver, while Maro busied herself with Seth and Jonny, fighting back her panic.

When they were on the train Tim offered to tidy her bag for her.

'You get in a muddle, Mum, because it's untidy – I'll sort it out and then we can go and have tea and I'll pay for it with your money, so you won't have to worry.'

Maro looked at Timmy's small serious face – I'm making him anxious she thought ... he's trying to look after me.

I'm sucking them into my spiralling terror. I must leave them for a bit – their grandmother would have them. She would calm them. She would kiss their foreheads instead of their lips. Yes, I'll go away for a bit.

'Tim, would you like to go and stay with Gran for a bit?'

'Yes,' said Tim. 'Yes, she'd let me look after the hens and the ducks and her pigs. Can Seth and Jonny come too?'

'Yes.' When I'm like this they want to get away from me. Yet how can I manage without them?

They had tea in the restaurant car, the table slowly becoming a wreck. Tea and milk swilling in the saucers and Jonny putting sugar lump after sugar lump into her teacup, so the paper melted off and floated to the top and the tea tasted of glue and dense sweetness, gripping the back of her throat, the bottom of the milk jug covered in raspberry jam and Seth's hair sticking in lumps with Jonny's chewing gum, and pieces of toasted tea-cake ground into cheeks and hands.

Back in their carriage someone was playing a transistor – 'Good Morning Starshine'. Jonny turning round in circles and clapping to the music, got dizzy, fell down and screamed. The screams were remote, far far away he seemed to be screaming, nowhere near her, and she stayed rooted in her seat unable to bend and pick up the screaming baby, her iron body unreal, non-existent ... till Tim picked him up and put him on Maro's lap. But this seemed to enrage him further. He twists in her arms and pokes his finger in her eye. All her eyelashes are thrust into her eye-ball and searing. She tried to put him on to the seat next to her but he bent himself backwards and went quite stiff and screamed still louder. She picked up his lorry but this only infuriated him more. Now he was hysterical and struggling. He crashed his head against her face.

A woman opposite offers him some Smarties out of a box, he hits the box as hard as he can and the Smarties, red, brown, yellow, mauve, fly all over other people's laps, scatter brightly across the floor strewn with cigarettes and old newspapers and spit. His rage grew to a mad struggling crescendo and he caught hold of the gold chain round her neck and pulled it tight so she began to choke. She tried to loose his gripping white fingers but he bent backwards flinging his taut little body against the chain and with his other hand entwining his fingers in her hair so she crouched forward over him, trying not to cry and he, even more enraged at her misery, screamed louder so she felt the whole carriage embraced and suffocated by his raging torrent and red-faced screaming. Suddenly he banged his head forward against her chest and bit hard into her bosom. She felt her face crack and tears running down, and then she began to feel she was going mad, slipping away from his blind impenetrable rage, slipping away from herself in a sliding dry avalanche, nothing to clutch, everything sliding, liquid, more and more distant, the rage in her ears and the pain of her pulled hair and bitten flesh.

The carriage was almost pitch-dark. I tried to see the children and the other people but they were frozen stiff and hazed together. I tried to get up but I couldn't move. I started sobbing. Tim was there putting his arms round me. 'My mind's melting,' I said. 'Where am I?'

'You're here, Mum,' said Tim.

'I know you're here, Tim, I can see you but I can't feel myself.' And I couldn't. I just had no feelings, no existence, it felt as if I wasn't there or anywhere ... as if I had no body, no spirit, nothing. I had 'gone round the bend'. I was 'lost', 'soft in the head'. 'Crazy.' 'Sunk.'

# PART TWO

Maro wasn't sure where she was but she knew she had been travelling for some time, partly on foot and partly by tube.

She remembered her mother-in-law coming to the house. She remembered her voice talking all the time like a full soft fruit – Don't worry, Maro – Have a holiday – You know the children are happy with me. Go abroad with your friends – I'll visit Ricci – Just rest.

The children had kissed her, excited to be going to the country – they had piled into the motor car and disappeared round the corner leaving her alone.

Now she was still alone but there were a lot of people around her and the noise of trains. She sat down on a bench. A brass band was playing, making the most deafening noise – a noise that wiped her out. Beside them was a collecting-box and a notice saying THE WESTERN REGION BRASS BAND. The music stopped and a voice crackled out over the loudspeaker, 'Will the carriage-train supervisor please call at the Aspen Road office.'

Maro made a vague attempt to get a grip on herself. 'Was that message for me?' The message came again. 'Will the carriage-train supervisor please call at the Aspen Road office.' It must be very urgent, thought Maro, I'd better go.

She got up off the bench and walked along the platform till she came to a photograph kiosk. WAIT THREE MINUTES AND THE PHOTOGRAPHS WILL BE DELIVERED OUTSIDE. 'I'll have my photograph taken and then I'll know if I'm the supervisor or not, in just three minutes. I hope they can wait three minutes.'

She stared into the machine and pressed the button, she sat and waited. The machine hiccuped and then like magic the pictures appeared.

They were amazing. She looked at them carefully and knew they were of a face she had seen before. It was a girl with hair down to her shoulders and a big mouth. She wasn't beautiful which disappointed Maro – she wished the girl was beautiful. She looked closer; it was a fascinating face, she couldn't stop looking. Hey, it wasn't by any chance the picture of a dog? The more she looked, the more like a saluki hound it became, ears and black nose. Am I a dog?

Outside the station there was a park. Maro walked among the trees. On a large oak was pinned a notice:

LOST

MY LITTLE BROWN-AND-WHITE ROUGH-HAIRED TERRIER WHITE FRONT AND LONG CURLY TAIL. I HAD HIM OUTSIDE MY HOME AT 2.15 A.M. TO RELIEVE HIMSELF AND JUST AS HE WAS COMING IN, THERE WAS A FLASH OF LIGHTNING AND HE RACED AWAY TERRIFIED.

IF FOUND PLEASE RETURN TO HIS HEART-BROKEN MISSUS (O.A.P.)

MISS BLIGH

FLAT 4, ARCASIUS ROAD, W.2.

GOOD REWARD

As she read it, wondering about Miss Bligh, a small dark-skinned woman with red hair, carrying a huge basket filled with vegetables, came up, read it and said,

'What a pity – what a *real* pity – white-fronted too! Well, I'll get Jim and Arthur to look for him this evening, they'll find him all right. A flash of lightning. Fancy that. You can never tell where you are these days.'

Maro went into the public lavatory. At the bottom of the steps she read IMPORTANT NOTICE, in large red letters:

> The public are requested to see the towels handed to them by the attendant are bound up in unbroken wrappers.
>
> W. E. Roberts
> Borough Surveyor

She started laughing. Near by sat a woman in a cubicle, drinking tea. She looked at Maro suspiciously. 'You could do with a cup of tea.'

'Yes,' she said, catching sight of her face in the mirror – What a frightened face – what terror-struck eyes …

She got her brush out of her pocket and started brushing her hair.

'It's threepence for a wash and brush up – see that notice,' said the lady.

'Oh sorry,' said Maro, putting her brush down on the table.

'Here you mustn't put that brush on my table – I eats my dinner off this table.'

'I'm sorry,' said Maro, looking closely at the attendant – 'Her face doesn't look frightened, perhaps she's got a good job.'

She looked round the polished cubicle. It looked cosy enough. Locker in one corner, small stove with a kettle on it. The chairs looked a bit hard. She sat down on the other one and the woman got a cup out of the locker, which she wiped on a towel.

Maro looked at her face in the brass rail; it curved curiously round the corner of the bar. As she moved it back and forth it got bigger and smaller.

'Are you hungry?' asked the woman.

'I don't know – what does it feel like?'

'Come off it,' said the woman pouring out the tea, 'think about your stomach ... '

Maro laughed. She began to feel happy as she thought about her stomach. First you were cold and your throat dry and slightly sick and your body felt light, each bone and muscle exposed, your gut and spine joined, and over all a longing to be invaded with warmth. What did the tea taste like, hot sour brew scalding my stomach.

'You can come back to my place and have a meal. I lock up soon.'

* * *

As Kitty unlocked the door a black mongrel puppy hurtled himself in the air and landed against her chest. She staggered backwards. 'Get down, sweetheart.' Next he leapt at Maro, his teeth catching in her coat.

It was a small concrete council flat, stuffed with rotting furniture and piles of second-hand clothes.

'He always is a bit bouncy when I get home of an evening – my husband's probably still in bed and not taken him out all day.'

There was a tap on the door.

'What is it?' shouted Kitty.

'I'm selling a pair of trousers.'

'What size?'

'I can't bring them down now because my leg's bad. I've got to bathe my bad leg.'

'I don't want them,' Kitty shouted back.

'Only yesterday that lady came down with a white fur cape. "Do you want to buy it?" she said. I gave her thirty bob for it. Why do people keep asking me to buy clothes when they know I haven't enough money for food? Grabbing and grasping. I could do some grabbing and grasping ... People are mad – they show off and forget all about the atmosphere.' She wipes her face on a pair of men's underpants. 'They're all glamour and patter. They're common and they're illiterate. My boy-friend, he was a nutcase, but he couldn't help it, he was torpedoed at sea. Ann Jones was rich – he was having sex with Ann Jones in Dean Street.

'My grandmother was called "the golden-haired beauty". She'd wet her hair and curl it round her finger and it would make one long curl. Very fascinating to men – she had a sexual look. She didn't talk much but she was crafty. She sat there listening, and the men liked it.'

'I'm making a scone,' she says. She mixes in a tin bowl a strange mixture of bread and marge and flour, adding water from a bowl marked DOG. She wears a pink dress with tiny pearls sewn round the neck and a long silk scarf tied round her neck at the side. And a green-and-white beret pinned on one side.

There is a terrible stench in the room and I can only hear half of what she is saying – the room is hazy and I feel dizzy.

'Highly polished like a romantic person's house. But my mother, she wouldn't give me any *hope* for anything. I pointed out a girl that was pretty. "I used to be like that, didn't I, mother?" "You *used* to be," she said.

'She made me leave the house in the pouring rain at

night – a man followed me at four o'clock in the morning. I was terrified. I had to walk round the streets in the rain and cold. She said she needed the room for a new maid.

'"We don't want you with your romances from London."

'He was bigger than me and broad – black curly hair. He knocked at my door. I was wearing a white satin dressing-gown and black satin shoes with feather boas on.

'He wanted me to be a film star but I hadn't the time. I was too busy.

'He threw me on the bed and started hugging and kissing me. Well of course I thought he was going to be the next prime minister. He took me to a girl's house. She was a student but I was jealous. There was something about Basil, any girl would melt. Of course I looked after him.

'I met this student on a bus. "Look," I said, "if you want a man I'll find you a man, but don't take mine."

'Then I found him in bed with a big Scotsman, with a red ribbon in his hair.

'I got hold of a chimney-pot and threw it through the window at him.

'He was escaping from me all the time.

'He was vain and he wanted the world like all politicians. He wanted me but then he wanted to go to someone else and be loved by them and then he'd always come back when he was tired.

'I suddenly created a longing for him and I thought, He's a long time out. I thought I'd go down to the beach and spring on his back and give him a surprise. But he wasn't on the beach – and I'd created such a longing for him.

'He told me to go out one day to the theatre – he always brought back lovely food from Romano's on the

Strand, chicken and glazed oranges. I didn't like cooking for myself. Then I found his handkerchief with lipstick on it. I followed him and saw him talking to a prostitute.

'I went to meet him one day and I saw this young woman waiting and I said, "What's your name?" and she said, "Mrs Macglrie", and I realized he must have got married.

'And then he came towards us and I thought he'd fling his arms around me and say "Kitty darling", but he walked straight past me and caught hold of her and said, "Look out for her, she's so jealous she'd cut your throat."

' "Cut your own throat, you old ponce," I shouted at him.

'But later when he was in hospital he cried his eyes out and said, "Now I haven't got my Kitty to go to bed with and keep me warm."

'There's something about me that can hold a man,' she said, her small blue eyes lighting up. 'I used to kick them, burn them with my cigarette – but they'd always come back for more.

'I had two girl-friends, one a beautiful big Irish girl, another wanted to sleep with me. She was a big tough girl with only one eye. She threw an American over the banister and broke his neck. He threatened to hit her.'

The soulful mongrel tied to the table leg by a piece of string. The 1930 wireless beating away. The fair-ground plaster ornaments piled on the piano. On the mantelpiece a picture postcard of the Queen and a birthday card of a red rose. A framed picture of a small boy saying his prayers. In a gold-rimmed glass, two battered Christmas crackers and a plastic tomato ketchup squeezer.

'He stole my jewellery. I was going down to Torquay to sort him out but he died before I got there, otherwise I would have smacked his face.'

She dries the dishes on the same pair of men's underpants that she had been wiping her face with. She lays out the plates on the table. The 'scone' is in the oven.

'I can sit and dream thousands of dreams. I have no regrets. If I go to the films they remind me of my life – when I hear them telling the girls they love them it all comes back to me, I recall the feelings, they all come back to me, the warm happy feelings.'

Maro felt lulled into this other life – she relaxed in spite of the smell and her dizzy mind.

'I had this woman-friend, she was rich. But she was very possessive. She wanted me all the time, body and soul. There and now. We used to have to tiptoe home through the night so she didn't see me. Once we couldn't get home; it was snowing. She fancied my husband. We'd lost our key so he rang the bell. She was making eyes at him through the letter-box but when she saw me she wouldn't open the door. She was very rich.'

The dog sat on her lap, his arms on her shoulders, constantly licking her neck.

'My dresses got covered in mildew – because she hung her wet washing just outside my bedroom window. She was a big blonde woman. Paid forty pounds for a coat and out she swaggered – she was all mouth and guesswork.'

The dog licks my toes, its mongrel-alsatian coat shining black and brown.

'She started a row with her sister's husband and drove him so mad that he opened the window and jumped out and broke his neck.

'I bought this television for three pounds ten. It hasn't got any sound or any picture but it's there, it only needs valves.

'My husband was kneeling on the floor making a milk

pudding. I was just teaching him to make one – we hadn't any furniture so we had to cook on the floor – when in she runs and knocks over the basin.

'My husband gets dizzy spells, that's why he stays in bed all day.'

The dog with its big stupid face jumped up at Maro and scratched her cheek. She hit its face and it yelped.

'Don't do that, you're cruel,' says Kitty.

Maro was frightened. 'I smacked his face because he kept jumping up at me.'

Kitty hugged the dog to her. 'It's all right, beautiful.

'It's because you're sitting in his place. That's his window-sill, he likes to watch the children play.'

She takes the dog's mouth very gently from her bag; this incredible gentleness makes Maro's heart ache.

Maro went to the lavatory. In the toilet is an enormous mop, its handle sticking up into the air. Maro pulled it out and it dripped all over the floor, so quickly she had a pee, pulled the chain and put it back.

'I had to hold him in my arms all night and feed him saucers of warm milk when someone kicked him in the street, it upset him so much.' Maro stroked him and Kitty brightened.

'I had this young Frenchman, he won beauty competitions for his looks. I've always had lovers – there's something about me that draws a man. When he left me he died.'

'Why did he die?'

'Because no one can look after them like I can.

'He was beautiful – long fingers, cut features. They take me out when my husband's asleep. I let one sleep on the chair one night but he pinched my husband's setting lotion.

'It was during the war, I had this flat up the West End. The landlord was killed by a bomb, so I didn't have to pay no rent for six months.

'They were all jealous of him in the West End, he looked so handsome. When he was dressed he looked dressed.

'I dress up and put the glamour on. I like red satin and I like furs.'

In the kitchen, in the cracked grey council fitted dresser – she opened it – no food, but stuffed with second-hand clothes from the glamour trade – peacock-green satin dress. She holds it up against herself. 'Sshsh, my husband's asleep in the bedroom, remember he has dizzy spells.'

The furs, the cracked gold turban hat.

'My husband and I we're very close, we go everywhere together.

'Our neighbour he painted CUNT outside our door to make it bad for us. I've had plenty of life, don't worry, and it was worth it. I've never wanted to own a house – I'd feel it was a prison. People with money, I have known lots of them – they get bogged down hanging on to things – they forget how to live.'

Maro staggered out into the air. So this was what living was about, now she knew. She wondered if she would ever make it.

I am learning to sleep sitting up on a hard bench – push your back against the bench, stretch your legs out in front of you and tuck your chin well in – let your eyes close slowly and you will fall into a light sleep, rich with dreams. There is one I keep having. I dream I am trying to sleep but every time I am falling asleep I am woken up to answer a question, but I can't ever answer it because I never know what the question is ... I just can never quite grasp the question.

Two teenage girls sit down beside me. They can't stop laughing and as they shake the bench vibrates and I too am rocked by their crazy laughter.

I walk along the road, a little brown mongrel follows me. She does a pee on a bit of newspaper and the remains of some grey chips and old fish-bones.

Standing on the corner is an Indian. 'Do you like Indian food – hot spicy food?'

I go into a cobbler's. He puts four metal pieces on my boots for sixpence. I stand barefooted in his shop.

'Did you go to the Isle of Wight to hear Dylan?' he asks. 'Did you get any free love?' The fat cobbler, his voice is gentle. 'I drove through France in my van but it's very dear there, it cost two pounds to go through the St Gothenburg tunnel.'

Outside was a tramp sitting on the kerb, holding in his hand a small green comb.

I wanted to be mad, neurotic, difficult, but they all expected me to be sane, normal, rational. 'She's such a good mother,' they said, but now I've done it, now I've shown them I'm bad ... Nowhere to go yet strangely free. Each hour my own. In the rain, sheltering in doorways, void space – difficult to decide anything, to remember who I am. Never mind, just forget, let the rain wash you away, soak into your face, trickle down your neck, it's getting difficult to move. Inside myself, get there slowly, ease there through all the rotten stench of fear. Gently shake it off. You really exist. Doorways of rubbish, broken windows, and blocks of flats standing like men with dead flesh, bolt upright and stiff. A big black man comes up to me and pinches my arm gently. 'She's a woman,' he says in a low voice, smiling right into my face, and then he walks away with a sloping easy stride.

I hear a tramp coughing and see a man stripped to the waist washing beside a caravan.

In the courtyard of a block of dwellings five small girls sit in a tight circle, chanting, 'Weeny, Tweeny, who's got the marbles?' They throw up their hands with excited bubbles of laughter. They are joined by another small girl pushing a push-chair in which sits a very dirty baby sucking a dummy. It is a still warm evening, one of them has a bottle of soda pop, a pigeon walks to a puddle to drink and a lean cat watches. The little girls quarrel and one tiny creature in a red dress jumps up and down making faces and lifting her skirt obscenely at the older girl, who stands in front of her angrily, hands on fat immobile hips.

The battered streets are touched with a halo of warm

sun, just a faint breeze and the birds singing.

I did used to feel sometimes but I never believed that feelings had any value. That what I felt could be important, rather than being totally disregarded and instead some rigid plan made out and dutifully followed.

She realized she had always wanted to be pregnant, because she felt so empty inside; she wanted to fill up the emptiness and this is why the sadness soon after birth.

The hunger for food – my belly roaring like a red-hot stove burning its last stick of food.

I go into a café. An enormous plate, piled, arrives. 'I couldn't eat all that.' 'I thought you looked hungry,' he says.

In the street a drunk woman weaves about and drops two bottles in the gutter.

'Where's your husband?' an Indian shouts to her.

'Which husband?' she shouts back.

In the monumental mason's stands a freshly inscribed stone – 'In Loving Memory of Louis Alberg. Deeply Mourned by his devoted Wife, Daughter, Son-in-law, Granddaughter, Brothers, Brother-in-law, Sister-in-law, Mechutanim, Relatives and Friends. May his dear soul rest in everlasting peace.'

There is a sweet smell of brewing beer, and flowers grow on a broken brick wall. A man with a yard brush sweeps water off the pavement. The sun is hot on the corrugated iron.

'Saleable By-gones Purchased', says a notice in a shop-window. A woman with swollen legs leans against the wall, waiting to cross, her two aluminium crutches under her arms, her feet swelling like weird growths out of her little-girl shoes.

Maro reads some more notices:

Urgent required
Perm. Resident.
Domestic Lady Aged 45–50 or Widow
(Own Room)
For Widower Pensioner Gent
Accidentally lost Both Legs
*No Nursing Required*

Barmaids Wanted.
Full and Part Time
Top Wages
Live in Sleep in or out.
Apply The College Arms.

She wondered vaguely if she should make some plans – but how to go about it she wasn't sure. She realized she had never had a job in her life and didn't know how to do anything to earn money, and the pile at the bottom of her bag was getting smaller.

A man and a woman walked past her, arms linked, carrying a heavy shopping basket. The woman held her face close to the man's as if to catch the warmth from his cheek. Maro felt immensely alone.

Sounds which before had just been a threatening noise which she had fought to shut out, one by one she began to distinguish them and their separate meanings. The sound of a child playing with a dog out on the muddy wasteland – it would be an ugly scruffy mongrel like Kitty's, with tail erect and ears pricked, barking at the boy, four square toes dug into the ground, making leaps into the air. And people – other people – had lives, had histories, had felt love and hunger and hate. They had faces and ears and mouths and strange noses and often their faces looked closed and sad. But sometimes they laughed. She looked with astonishment at the faces of children, one girl of about nine sitting on a bench with her mother, her long brown hair in two smooth bunches, her straight-fringed and perfect little face. She wore a cherry dress. Maro remembered her grandmother ...

My grandmother telling me how her mother died when she was twelve. Her maid, Miss Pike, asked her which dress she wanted to wear and when she chose the cherry said, 'You can't wear that one, your mother died in the night.' And she had had no idea her mother was even ill.

Two old men come along the street carrying an enormous bale of rags, one in front, the other behind. The front one stops by me. 'Hello Margaret, how are you keeping?' The back one, who can't see what is going on, starts yelling, 'Come on then, what yer doing, come on, get on ... '

Maro laughed and the man laughed too as he went on his way.

A fat old lady sat down next to her. 'Hello,' she said. One shoe-lace was missing and she wore a dirty camel-hair coat. 'I had a sheep-dog for fourteen years. When my husband died last year he fretted so much I had to have him put to sleep. Oh, I do miss him, he was a lovely dog.'

'What about your husband?' asked Maro.

'He was all right till he retired, then he started driving me mad. I couldn't even get to the sink but he was in the way – following me about all day, enough to drive a woman mad having a man around you twenty-four hours in one room. I began to envy widows ... Now I'm going to tell you something that will really surprise you – hang on for a shock.'

Maro waited. 'Before he died I hadn't had any married

life for ten years!' She heaves a sigh and shuts her mouth waiting for Maro's amazement.

'It's not my fault,' she goes on, 'I'm sexually perfect, always have been and always will be. It's him, he couldn't make it stand up with iron bars and you know it makes your nerves bad cooped up with a man who can't do anything ...'

Maro had a sensation of extreme lightness. Her head felt empty, her feet were hardly touching the ground – she sauntered on around each corner, down each street, reeling with a sensation of freedom so overpowering as to wipe out all guilt or anxiety.

She met the night, for the first time, the night, the moon, the badly lit streets, the cool empty night, and as she listened the night became full, rich, extraordinary, alive with sounds, a quiet pulse; she tuned in to the night. She felt like some country that had been oppressed for a long time and was slowly rising up and throwing over its oppressors. She was making a revolution but the bloodshed was horrifying, and how many lives would be lost and where was it going to end and would she ever make the country of the free spirits?

Through a broken doorway she heard voices and saw the light of a bonfire. She went towards it. A gathering of people sat around – all women except for one oldish man. A slender young woman with very blonde hair and high black boots greeted her.

'Hello love, come and sit down.' She made room on a wooden box. The conversation continued, leisurely, spacious. The man got up to throw more wood on the fire, his name was Sid. He offered Maro a humbug. She sat by the flames sucking her warm humbug, wrapping her knees in her coat and feeling the cool night air blowing her cheeks.

She sat close to Jeany with her high-heeled boots and sweet rich smell – a kind of scented sexual smell, of powder and Woolworth's and moments of unwashed ecstasy.

'I remember my first wedding anniversary at Number eleven. My husband was away of course and Tom climbed up the drain-pipe and was sitting on my bed when I woke up. We talked all the rest of the night. He brought me three pairs of drawers in a box with a little heart in it, and a pink pair with a black fringe but they wore out. Before I knew Tom I wore white aertex drawers.'

'That's what they always made us wear in the nut-house,' said Annie in her deep croaky voice. 'Nerve hospital,' corrected Sid. 'Well, "nerve hospital", it's all the same isn't it? That's where Sid and I met. Remember in '45? We did that dance. You loved dancing. You would have gone on all night. Like this, you went ... '

Annie gets to her feet. She is very short and wide with long tangled brown hair. She starts stamping about. One, two, three – bang. She sings, 'Dadada da da', as she stamps in a circle.

'What is it about me that makes people stop me and ask the way – why am I always the centre of attraction? I haven't done anything to anyone?' Sid asks. 'Only today someone asked me the way to Tottenham Court Road and I said, "Why do you pick on me?"' Sid with his worn-out blue suit.

Annie stopped dancing and sat down again next to Sid. 'I dreamt about you. I could see your legs hanging from the curtain.'

'Was it only my legs you could see?'

'Yes, only your naked legs hanging down.'

'Well, that's all right if you could only see my legs,'

says Sid. 'I've never done anything improper – I've never thought it worth while doing anything improper.'

'Heh, what about that time you said you was going to mend yer bike in the bathroom ... and I goes in there with him and we locks the door but of course they can see us through the frosted glass. When I come out the doctor gets hold of me and says, "This place isn't a brothel – you'll go to Number nine and you'll like it." Number nine was a locked ward and I was in there six months without seeing Sid.'

'Poor Annie,' says Jeany. 'They put me in the N.H. once. It nearly drove me mad. I didn't sleep all night. When the early morning come I slept but then I was woken by the trains going past. After a week me nerves were standing on end. I was exhausted but I still couldn't sleep. Now when I was with Tom, that's when I could get a night's sleep. It was like being drugged, we'd both go off – thick deep sleep that you never wanted to wake up from.'

An old woman sitting near the fire started to cough. 'You wouldn't sleep much in Hopetown I can tell you. Somebody in the dormitory had a heart attack last night, that's what's put me off.'

'Don't worry, Rita. It'll need more than a heart attack to finish you off.'

Maro looked at the stars and remembered Seth saying, 'When the world blows up, will the stars still be there?'

Rita was talking to her. 'I injured my spine thirty years ago. So I can't bath – it's arthritis I've got – I have to wear this.' She pulls out of her bag a broken piece of sorbo rubber partly covered in grey stockinette.

'Have you got lodgings?' she asks Maro. 'Perhaps we could share. Would you like to share with me? Perhaps we could get a nice furnished room. Tomorrow I'll look in the *Hackney Gazette*. I've got a widow's pension. I don't go to work, I've never troubled to look for a job. It's all centrally heated in the hostel but it's not rosy, it's not like a fire, not really rosy in the dormitories in there. You get a lot of people with asthma in there, they breathe very heavily in the night, keeps you awake. My husband died of alcohol and cancer. Of course you can't wash your clothes in the hostel, only your underclothes, there are women been in there ten years haven't been allowed to wash their frocks.

'And you can't stay in bed after nine, oh no, even if you're dead you've got to get out. I told the captain, "I've got a chill," I said.

' "Don't come to me with your aches and pains," she said. "This isn't a hospital." ' Once again Rita was enveloped in coughs. She pulled a small bottle out of her pocket and took a swig.

'That's better – this is marvellous linctus the nuns give yer.'

'Give us a swig, Rita,' says Annie. The bottle is passed round. Maro takes some.

'Remember Granny?' asks Jeany, 'She had this black fridge, it opened pink ... it was beautiful and a big brass bowl on top ... you used to get your tip left in that ... she had this boy-friend George. Wow! he just looked money, you should have seen the rings on his fingers. I could have had him off of her. I bet he had a great place ... '

'I couldn't live in a house,' says Annie. 'I think houses are like prisons. Then everybody comes around making you feel inferior because your place isn't done out as good as theirs.'

'I've often thought when I retire,' says Jeany, 'I'll go out with a bang. Get a luxury flat, lie on the bed and eat chocolates.'

'That's it, when yer time comes you've got to retire and make way for someone else.'

'But I don't want to be forgot ... I'd like people in the street to turn round and say, "She could fuck years ago." I'd have that on my tombstone. SHE WAS A GOOD FUCK. In great big fancy letters.'

'That's it, Jeany,' says Annie, 'live now while you've got the chance. Once I had a terrible row with my husband. "You dirty whore," he calls me. "So I'm a whore, am I?" I says. "Well, next time I'm fucking some bastard at least I'll be paid for it." '

'I don't know why you can't settle down like any other young lady,' says Sid.

'Settle down. That's what all men say because they're terrified of us being alive. What they really mean is buckle under and turn into their slave. Don't give me that, Sid. We are born alone, we live alone, we die alone.'

'I don't know,' says Annie, 'I believe that somewhere in the world there exists my twin star, but how ever can I find him?'

'What's wrong with me, then?' says Sid.

'Perhaps you're better off without him. Look at me – my life's one long honeymoon. Jack's going to take me on holiday to Spain when his ship comes home. I'm going to wear a coffee-coloured blouse, long cream skirt and tight jacket. Have me photo taken sitting by the seaside wearing a cream-coloured beret on me blonde hair ... '

'And what'll you do if his ship doesn't come home?' asks Rita.

'Ah well,' says Jeany, 'I'll stick around here.'

Annie laughs. 'Watch yourself if a man finds out you're two-timing him ... '

'Two-timing him? Who owns me body? I'll have ten

men if I want to – they're free to come and go. Nobody keeps me ... I like blokes ... the day I'm going to start worrying is the day when I can't stand them any longer. If you start hating people ... if you start getting bitter, you get ugly, your skin gets coarse, but while you're in love you're beautiful.'

'Here, I haven't seen your friend black Mick for weeks.'

'No, he's gone to America. I went to see him off at the airport, there was fog and the planes were grounded, the bar was full. You know how they look at a white girl and black man. I had this red silk dress that shows all me cracks up. As you breathe it shows all yer tits up ... They were all crushing against us and he put his face up against mine and he was saying all these passionate things and everybody could hear and I didn't care and he bought this bottle of perfume and he was smearing it all over my face and neck, putting his fingers down my dress all covered with this sweet scent ... '

'It's the foreign blood ... it heats you up ... ' says Annie ... 'When I was young I was working in a hotel, there was this Italian waiter – Frank, his name was – I was always running after him. He was a darling. I was a chamber-maid and he was a waiter. He wasn't allowed to come to my room and I wasn't allowed to go to his – so we used to have it in the coffee lounge. It was his job to clean up the coffee lounge when everybody was finished and left. I used to meet him there – he wore one of them little dicky bow ties and black tail-coat – I was crazy for him. We'd only had it seven times when I began to feel sick. I think I'm having a baby, I told him. He didn't seem to worry. We went on meeting in the coffee lounge and having it till I was about six months and my belly had got very big – then they sacked me. I went to my brother who took one look at me and said, "Who did that to you?"

'Well, he went to the hotel and tried to find Frank. But Frank, the artful bugger, had left. I never saw him again. Still, why worry ... I like the unknown ... About ten years ago I met my husband in the road. "Hello Bob!" I said.

'He looked straight through me. "Don't speak to me. I'll have you arrested," he said.'

This was Annie, Annie who got married to a soldier in the war and never saw him again. Never saw him in his demob suit but found out he'd collected it.

Maro fell into a half-sleep. Images of dragons and fierce monsters raved through her head in strange procession. Awake, and yet dreaming night-sleep dreams, while the flames leapt and Annie laughed and Rita complained and Sid moved slowly about collecting wood and Jeany sat close to her for warmth.

What are these people to me? Only strangers and I am lonely and yet I am free. Free to be lonely. Free to be sad. The smell of strange bodies, strange cultures and voices. Is this the brotherhood of the soul? Away from the suffocating atmosphere of furniture and lined curtains and people who call you by your name – who call you by your name and expect you to be good.

'You don't need much to stay alive,' says Annie. 'Just a bun and a cup of tea every four hours.'

It was a wet dark windy day. Maro didn't know where any of her new-found friends were.

You didn't ask questions. There was no possessiveness about people here – they came and went, they were free spirits to whom plans and appointments were like prison bars.

She was hungry and knew she had hardly any money left.

She started walking. Loneliness came over her in great waves. The wind blew in wet and dirty gusts round each corner. A boy ran with two black mongrels loping beside him. She didn't want to stop walking in case she felt too lonely to start again; if she stopped walking she thought she might sink to the bottom of the sea.

She saw a fat old woman standing in a doorway. As she came up the woman spoke to her.

'Please Miss, my light's gone and I daren't stand on the chair ... please could you help me.' Maro went in. It was a tiny dark room.

'Sit down,' said Maro. 'I'll put the new bulb in.'

'There's one in the toilet.'

I went and fetched a bulb from the toilet in the back-yard and when I came back there she sat in the dark, her hat and coat still on, in the quiet. I put the bulb in and the room lit up brighter and yet cold and empty.

'Oh thank you,' she said and struggled to her feet and clasped me in her arms. She sobbed and heaved and told me she was lonely. An old ship in an ocean – a cold wide ocean – her body was so heavy and soft clinging to mine.

'HAPPY is the Bride who wears a Leyton Wedding Ring,' said a notice in a shop selling crucifixes and contraceptives.

Two women pushed past me, talking.

'So when he dies he'll have no stone – I'm not going to put a stone on him – serve him right.'

A fat young man comes up to me. 'Here darling, I've got something I want you to analyse.' He holds a bloody syringe. I look at it. 'Do you know where I found it? I found it in my arm.'

How disgusting it is here, the hundreds of squawking chickens in crates down the narrow dirty street. The meat stall with bloody pieces of hacked corpses hanging in the window. Any minute someone will jump out and drag me into one of those festering doorways. Rubbish and heavy air full of odour.

I stop and ask a woman with a shopping basket the way to East Street, where I believe there is a hostel. Suddenly I want a bed, I want hot water to wash my hands. But she is hysterical – full of raving fear at my question. 'I don't know, I don't at all, I'm sure I don't know. No, I don't know ...'

At last I find it, down a dark passage, there is a door at the end. I knock.

Inside are about twenty middle-aged women – the strangest assortment you ever saw. The one who opened the door had two rolling eyes, they rolled round and round like mad marbles without anchors. Another was so fat she could only stagger.

'Have you a bed for tonight?'

'Oh no! No!! No! There are no spare beds here.'

'Well, can I use your toilet please?'

I was shown through into the back-yard where there was a row of four toilets with half-doors and a corrugated iron roof and rain trickling down inside the walls. Beside them was a wooden bench, pots of flowering plants, beautiful azaleas and marigolds and forget-me-nots under glass cloches. I came back into the big dark room.

Chairs stand in rows, tight side by side in front of the telly. And this strange bunch of women, great fat ones with long grey hair, and flat ones as if they'd been ironed out under a steam roller, sit upon them.

'May I sit down for a moment, I've come a long way,' I say.

'No dear. No love. Sorry, you can't sit down here.'

I stare blankly around at all the empty chairs. 'No dear. No love.' Hurrying me towards the door.

Crazy terrifying city, now the wind is wild. How to keep on wading through this rubbish dump? I am cold, I am hungry, I have no money, is this freedom?

As she walked along past lighted windows she kept seeing fresh corpses hanging from the ceiling in each room. When she looked closer they disappeared. In the street, all the cars looked as if they carried coffins but pretended not to.

In the station waiting-room an old man was being sick on the floor ... soon two policemen appeared. 'Come on, Harry, get moving.' They dragged him to his feet. He staggered like Ricci and groaned.

'Where can I sleep tonight?' Maro asked one of the policemen. 'I've only got two shillings.'

'St Joseph's. You get the tube to Liverpool Street and then ask. The nuns will look after you.'

'Thanks,' said Maro. She watched the staggering Harry and thought of Ricci ...

It really doesn't make much difference ... it's just another of society's crazy ideas that everybody should be the same – so what if you can't walk, you can usually do something else like sing or watch birds ...

In the gloomy silent wastes of Aldgate East Station a blind man taps his way along the platform. He comes to a pillar and makes his way round it, heading directly for the drop and the live rails. A man on the other side shouts, someone whistles, but they don't get to him in time. Over he goes like a toy soldier in the front line.

I sweat with fear, my heart beats fast – I must get to a bed, I must sleep, I must wash my face in hot water.

* * *

It was an enormous brown room. A young woman in her bra sits up in bed holding a weeping child. The nun stops by her. 'You mustn't cry you know, naughty boy, you're not allowed to cry in here.' Women, huge bulky ships wrecked in the mud. Large ungainly forms under the bedclothes and a terror, a terror of the good nuns inquiring gently where you went wrong.

'We can let you stay here a few days till you get on your feet.'

But how did you get on your feet? she wanted to ask them.

People are broken chattels, all broken, lost, in pieces, all searching, no, most here have given up the search, they have gone into a world where they neither love nor expect love. Hulks washed up on the beach. Sunk ships beyond repair, left to rot on the shore, washed by the waves until they die and then their carcasses are burnt.

The nun showed her to a bed. On either side, quite close, were other beds. In all, the rooms must have held about sixty women and children.

The old woman on her right was sitting up searching in a paper bag. She looked at Maro.

'See my hair, there's not a hint of grey in it and I've never done a thing to it.' Maro looked in mild surprise at the old woman's grey hair.

'I had a man stop me the other night. "Come home with me and I'll warm you up," but I was frightened. I thought he might outrage me, there are plenty of dirty men about. Even in Southend I've had offers from men.'

'Would you like a sweet?' asked Maro, offering a barley sugar.

'No, thank you. No. No. It makes me feel inferior. I always feel inferior, if I have any comfort I feel uncomfortable. Why should I have anything given to me? I'd rather sleep on a park bench. The time when I really feel best is when they lock me in my cell at Holloway and I think, Well, that's it – this is my cell, bare, nothing – now no one can get me down any further.'

The light is dim. Maro fills the wash-basin with warm water. It is behind a wooden screen open at both ends on to the room. She lays her hands in the basin, the warmth runs up her arms. She takes off her boots and trousers and washes her feet.

Maro gets into bed. The little child has fallen asleep. Outside it is still daylight – she wondered why they all went to bed so early. The room was quiet. She shuts her eyes and longs for sleep ...

Because, you know, I suffer from night desolation, my youngest son suffers from it too. It happens about three o'clock in the morning when the bed is lonely – sometimes he wakes too and then I can drag him out of bed and into mine and the warmth of his small limbs restores me to life. Otherwise I feel death rise up all around me, the air is thick with ghosts and I am alone. If only I could love everybody in this room like the nuns do. But I find it hard to love people. Why am I so bad at living? Oh wind that shakes the body free.

Later the room trembled with groans and murmurs – a kind of heaving agony of the earth as if warning of a quake. The night was alive with sorrow – voices speaking in sleep, and coughing from the very guts. Maro hung on to herself against the wave of desolation that rose up from these semi-sleeping bodies.

Across the room she saw a naked figure, its flesh white and heavy, leaning over a basin, retching.

Maro tried to force herself to go to her but she was pinned to her bed by misery and terror.

'Perhaps she wouldn't want me to see her naked ...'

She heard the woman sobbing, great retching sobs. She sat naked on the floor under a dim bulb, sobbing and wiping her eyes on her white arm.

Maro went to her and crouched beside her, offering a barley sugar in the palm of her hand as if to a wild horse. The woman went on weeping, great heaving quaking tears running down her face. Maro started to cry too. She put her arms round the woman's neck and cried; burying her face in the large drooping bosom, she cried and cried and the woman cried too. She realized she hadn't cried since she was about twelve and it was as if her rotten heart had burst open like a bad fruit.

Later she slept and dreamt she had multiple sclerosis and could move nothing except her head.

# PART THREE

G

Maro had spent the last pennies that she found in the bottom of her bag – the source she had imagined was endless – on a bath.

In a great old-fashioned bath she had sunk her body – she had washed her hair and her underclothes. And now, clean again, carrying her pants and bra in a wet ball in her hand and wearing only trousers and a jumper under her rabbit-skin coat, she left the steamy atmosphere for the street. She went east towards the river and walked down the slimy stones to the water, where she saw a young man collecting driftwood.

'Hi,' he said, carrying a great armful of wood on to a half-sunk barge. 'What are you doing here?'

'I'm trying to find somewhere to dry my underclothes.'

'There's a stove on the barge, I'll show you.'

He led the way over a tiny gang-plank, turning round to catch hold of her hand to steady her and then let it go.

Inside was a glowing stove and a bed and a long wooden room with tools and books and a view along the muddy beach.

'Sit down and dry your things while I finish collecting the wood. My name is Daniel.'

Later when it got dark he took her out on to the beach

and ran along the stones, dragging her after him, stumbling and screaming at him to stop. He climbed an old post, thick with green slime, in his bare feet, and hung on a rope from his hands above the filthy water. The whole place stank from the large carcass of a cow half-rotten below him.

All the way back he kissed me. He kissed me as we balanced, leaping from boulder to boulder to avoid the smooth clinging mud. Daniel, wide broad large eyes, thick mouth, broad back, a kind of heaviness about him.

He kissed me all the way up the gang-plank, and I was only frightened, frightened about falling into the water.

On the barge he stopped kissing me and asked if I wanted something to eat.

'Yes, I'm hungry.'

He got oats – 'ninepence' it said on the packet – and milk and syrup and filled two bowls and set them on the table and we ate.

'You can sleep here,' he said. 'Get into bed.'

While she undressed, he washed the bowls and spoons and put away the oats, carefully folding down the top of the packet.

Then he washed himself in cold water, dipping his head right into the water and blowing it out of his mouth and shaking his head. When he got into bed his face was still wet. He kissed her, pressing his wet face against her body.

How alive he was, that was all she could think about, this overwhelming energy bursting from each throbbing pore of his body. His flesh pressed against her, close, close up against her.

Hugging, slow, gentle, sweet, pressing into me wider

and wider, he puts his hands round the inside of my thighs, pressing my legs open.

He bent my knees up, hooking them round his arms and lay his stomach between my legs, rocking gently back and forth, his hard belly rubbing backwards and forwards on my open cunt.

'I have money to get us to Europe,' said Daniel. 'After that we'll hitch and when we've spent all I've got I'll sing and you can collect.'

Now they were on a train. She had half hoped he would disappear so she could avoid the emotion of seeing him and being with him – she didn't want to have to feel. But he was there, and now he sat opposite her in the carriage, asleep. Jean-clad legs spread out, thick wrists with black hair, thick hair, big mouth, looking a bit grey and exhausted after no sleep.

She wondered why she had come – she didn't like travelling with strangers.

In the carriage two ladies in their seventies sat next to one another, quarrelling over who had forgotten the thermos, and eating sweets out of an old-fashioned jar. One reads *The Guardian* and the other a novel ... 'My word,' says the one with *The Guardian*.

Maro felt black with tiredness, all she wanted was to go to sleep.

They found a corner on the open deck against the rails. Daniel made a seat for her with the sleeping-bags and his rucksack to lean against. She wanted a cup of tea but he fetched her water. 'Taste it,' he said, 'it's better than tea.' He sat beside her, played his guitar and sang her a beautiful song:

'Water, water, see the water flow,
Glancing, dancing, see the water flow,
Oh wizard of changes
Teach me the lesson of flowing.'

She slept, her hands tucked under her stomach for warmth. The sleep was a crazy journey into a dark wood and out again and she half slept, singing 'Happy Birthday to you, Happy Birthday to you,' over and over again. Happy Birthday to the Black Night of her mind and the sleep quietened her soul.

Later he kissed her, bending her back over the wooden railing.

Everything is reversed, the sky and the stars upside down and the rolling waves showering my face.

'I want to open you up,' he said. He was breaking her open. 'Let yourself go.' Shaking her pelvis loose, letting it down, down, till she thought her back would break and her head would drop off. Blood flooding round her body – down her legs, into her fingers, little tremors running up her thighs, everything stretching, opening. She began to feel dizzy and couldn't move. He lifted her up and she collapsed at his feet.

'That's an exercise,' he said, 'to make you come alive.'

* * *

Our first night of camping after sleeping two nights on the boat. Fifteen miles south of Corona. We turned up a stony track just as it was getting dark and found an abandoned cottage with no roof and a grassy footpath leading down to a bubbling stream. Stony ground, with olive groves across the valley and in the distance mountains, overhead, stars. We had zipped the two sleeping-bags together and found a flat piece of ground, carefully clearing the stones away.

I caught his hair and pulled it, pulling down his face and never-stopping kisses, the heat from his lips burning my sore cheek. Sore with the hair on his chin growing every minute, as his face moved from side to side against mine, as his kisses fell like hot rain on my sore cheeks, hot sweet kisses bursting like sparks from fireworks, lit up by his body all over mine so soft, so warm all over mine, like a warm sea breaking over the beach of my body, exploding into laughter, lying shaking across my heart, sobbing or laughing, I couldn't tell. And when I asked him he said, 'It's all the same, really.'

In the morning the sun, the clamour of clear-headed birds, peasants on their way to work, a woman leading an ox, a priest riding on a donkey followed by two goats. Climbing out of the sleeping-bag and walking down to the stream to wash. Standing in the water, the cool water splashing round my legs, the flowers in the undergrowth, the lizards scattering over the flat stones, rustling through the leaves and brambles, tadpoles round my toes.

I can understand for the first time the way gypsies can't live in houses, after living in the open – the world belonging to you, the flowers, the stones, the smell of the fresh minty air. The sun, time, my body, all belong to me. People try to tell you, your body and your time belong to someone else. The wine, the sweet oranges, the smell of crushed mint underfoot. Daniel brings me over a giant snail to see, and wanders off. Soon he calls me to watch a lizard on a rock and point out a tadpole in our drinking water.

That night he tells me about the stars till I fall asleep.

* * *

'You're still stiff,' he said. 'Watch this.' He put the folded sleeping-bags over a low stone wall. Then he flung himself backwards across it. His head and shoulders and arms hung upside-down the other side and his hips and legs dangled beside me. 'Now you,' he said, getting up. He made me do it – it hurt and my legs stuck straight out in front of me. He pushed at my hips. 'You see how stiff you are – you are armoured, closed, unable to really feel sexually and give yourself sexually to anyone.'

And after last night he could say that.

* * *

Waking to feel the first hint of sun filtering through the oak trees. I never knew there were oak trees in Spain.

And so the world became real. The heat and the cold, her knees, but most of all her spine – he made her spine into a live snake linking up her belly and limbs to her brain.

The thick dew on the ground, my hair is wet – getting the stove going to make the boiling hot coffee and eating a chunk of mozzarella out of some damp brown paper. All along the road, eating oranges and waiting for a car to stop.

The insects in the grass, the caterpillars crawling across the sleeping bag. And so he teaches me to look now. Look at the brown-and-yellow caterpillars, feel the sun on your cheek, examine the stones on the ground beside you. Look at the grass by the stream and the little yellow-and-purple wild orchids.

One night we slept in a grove of wild mimosa, a hundred yards from the sea. Wild flowers clustering thickly round our little camp where I was boiling water in the blue pan.

Saw a black snake while walking down a path into the wood. Woke up with mimosa blossom dropping on to our faces. We swam in the cold sea.

Daniel, after carving our names on a mimosa tree, is wandering about collecting flowers which he is pressing in a copy of *Anna Karenina* – so far he has found seventeen different kinds.

* * *

Washing our clothes in the sea, letting the waves slide over the hole in the sand. My red ribbon and silver whistle hanging round my neck ready to call Daniel if the mussel-collecting man, with his brown neck and rolled-up trousers, comes too close.

That night when he had finished with her she felt so bashed, battered, cracked, broken, split open, her whole body ached. She slept for ten hours and woke up still exhausted, floating time, held spun, stretched.

I remember once I came upon Ricci sitting on a grassy bank throwing nuts to lambs; it was the first sunshine of April, hot enough to sit out of the wind. I caught his pure delight full in the face – he alone, the grass, the sun, the lambs close upon him, eager for the nuts – he was happy there, he loved that place – he dug it all, he had feelings. Why did he never tell me about them?

* * *

We were sitting on the grass, eating biscuits and marmalade.

'I wouldn't ever climb into a coffin,' I said.

'I don't suppose you'll ever have to climb into one,' he said. 'Oh Dan,' I said, and fell towards him. He held me laughing and when I drew back he showed me where I had put marmalade all over his nipple and arm. I licked it off remembering how I had licked the milk and Rice Krispies off Jonny's leg – in his rage he had flung them at me.

The strange ballet of sex, crushing and opening, opening and melting, wider, wide.

Later he lay on me and his sweat trickled down my ribs in warm dribbles and I loved him, shuddered beneath his weight and heat, and loved him.

Yet do I really care for him? Sometimes it seems like acting in a play.

I looked at the photographs of his parents and his home, they were so terrible, his house a concrete box with iron-barred window-frames like a prison.

'Your parents, they never made it, they never made the trip to one another, they never melted, did they?'

He looked at me in astonishment. 'How did you know?'

He sobbed, quaked, quaked in my arms, shook.

I always *thought* with my head if I loved someone. Loved them for all their attributes and kissed them, thinking of their attributes in my head. And now I begin to feel, to be aware of a warmth in my belly when Dan strokes my knees.

But then the warmth in my belly doesn't connect with my brain, so is this one of the endless misconnections? I can actually feel the warmth leap away from my belly into my brain when I start to talk. It is true you have to be quiet a bit to be aware of your feelings – keep silent a moment or two – But are feelings really worth keeping silent for? Are they really worth having?

* * *

We are in a large modern station. Daniel is singing and I must walk up to the hurrying people with the blue enamel cup and ask for money – we are totally without it. A man bumps up against me and I sweat – sweat with fear from the rough contact.

Dan sang:

> 'My greatest friend a song has given
> To sing where I may go,
> To sing among the green green hills
> And where the waters flow.'

And men and women gave me money. In Spain people aren't so embarrassed about giving money to beggars. They gave me money and looked at me with curiosity and even tenderness.

> 'The waters from that wondrous well
> That made my eyes to see,
> And made my Mind to ever show
> My greatest Friend to me.'

And every day there was the exercise – tipping her back over logs or banks or walls. Tipping her back, back and the blood flooding her brain and her spine stretching and her stomach letting go and such a feeling of openness and softness welling over her, submerging her ... making her want to lift her knees and stretch her legs wide open.

But sometimes the pain was enormous and she thought, Perhaps my spine will snap and I will be Incurable.

* * *

Dan crouching by the river looking at the stones and the water washing the seaweed-green fine hair back and forth in little curls over the stones.

He fills me with nervous energy and never satisfies me – he gropes towards me and I grope towards him, the neurotic feels through a chink but what he feels or sees is blinding and he searches afterwards in vain – for the same vision.

He is squeamish, appalled by dirt, obsessed by food. At three o'clock in the morning I wake up and find him sitting in the moonlight eating oats.

His body flung on to mine is heavy, it crushes me. I give up under his weight, under his flesh – I am wiped out.

The next morning, senseless after only two hours sleep, I get up a sleep-walker, only calm when exhausted. I get up like a punch-drunk boxer from his corner, reeling yet ready for the next round. What possible outcome is there for me in this battle?

He puts his lips against mine and keeps them there for a long time.

'We do battle together,' he said. 'You are my equal.' We talked of 'risk', of the risk of helping the mad and the maimed and of risking one's own sanity, and Dan said until you had made yourself strong and happy you should not do it and I said you had to because what else is there except television and chocolates.

His body beating against mine until I am nearly unconscious, a wave beating against the rocks.

My body sucked into his, his into mine, and afterwards the smell of scorched flesh, scorched burnt flesh.

Sometimes she wished they belonged to one another.

How to choose a man and say, 'Well, this is he, and too bad about all the others I cannot have.'?

She remembered the married man's words: 'Sometimes I feel I've totally failed by being neither faithful to my wife nor mistress.'

Dan says, 'It depends how much you love somebody's spark, somebody's soul.'

His bones press against mine, only a thin layer of skin separates us – he grinds my bones, his mouth on my mouth. He opens me by his attacks.

'It's that you must give yourself the chance to have a whole relationship – never mind too much if, in the end, it's bad or good, as long as you can give the whole of yourself to it – you're always avoiding giving yourself. Holding back, holding back.'

'But', I say, 'perhaps I don't exist and there's nothing there to give.'

When this morning he suddenly turned and gathered me up into his arms, pressing me to him, I felt my stomach and bones melt, just melt, into a hot streaming fluid – it was such a physical feeling. I felt it in my body, instead of just in my heart or brain. That I actually had feelings like other people!

* * *

Walking through the forest, marking our path with bits of wood so we find the way home – the enormous beeches and oaks – the dead cow in the pond gasping for breath, mouth open, sides heaving in the moment of death. I wish I were a Siamese twin – what unbelievable intimacy.

In the middle of the night – always my most desolate time – I get a tiny splinter of glass in my big toe. Dan helps me get it out. 'If it gets in your bloodstream it can go to your heart,' he says. And then he falls asleep and I lie in the warm nest, legs in the warm against legs – flesh against flesh, body to body – do I want the constancy he is offering me – no, I think, I could never really bear to 'belong' to any man and yet the world is so lonely and the night most lonely of all. And what would I do with no one to take the glass out of my toe, perhaps I would die.

He says, 'I just want to live, that is the summit of my ambitions.'

* * *

Remember, remember this afternoon and him running out of the glistening sea in front of you, running towards the trees, the mountains beyond him, his feet bombing along on the hard sand, his brown back glistening, his hair wet and clinging to his neck, remember, remember, full of love for him, full, full up and bursting with love for him, as you struggle behind, knee-deep in the salty sea, hair in wet locks around your ears, water running down your face, the late afternoon sun low over the mountains.

Remember how later that night your mouth clung to his mouth, and he held you tight, tight and you sucked at his lips and pushed your cheek hard, hard against his cheeks and dissolved away, away, melted away in his clinging arms. Remember when you opened your eyes, the moon was sickle-fine and the stars of the Plough were just above your heads.

That night I felt like the snow that fell upon the beach at Llandudno and was washed away by the waves.

* * *

When they got to Morocco they travelled by train, and the days got hotter and the countryside got browner and so did the people. Women wore coloured dresses and tied yellow and pink scarves round their heads, and there were clusters of mud-walled houses and small yards with hens and a woman lifting over her shoulder a bare-bottomed laughing tot, and a river bounded by yellow flowers and bamboos and in the distance the mountains, and Daniel constantly at her to do her bending exercises over the edge of train seats, in the corridors, when they stretched their legs at stations or got out to drink from the 'L'eau potable' tap. Made her bend her neck till it ached, and stretch her spine and breathe deeply while the fields went by and three little girls skipped in the dust by a small railway siding with an orange grove behind. And a whole forest of eucalyptus and giant cacti dwarfing the straw-thatched huts and mud-thatched hay stacks – and now and then they drank mint tea and dipped the bread they had bought in the hot sweet brew. And out of the window she saw a lad on a grey horse galloping against a bare brown hill.

Maro was smiling and then she was laughing. This sensation of happiness creeping up on her and into her face. It seemed a long time since she had laughed, as if her face had gone stiff, rigid, and to laugh she had to crack it open – but now out of the window she saw mules up to their knees in muddy water and a man with an oar who seemed to be rowing himself along.

'Look,' she said, 'he hasn't a boat,' and she laughed and frightened herself with the noise of her laughter and started to sweat.

They got out of the train and walked across a dusty space. An old storyteller, his face burnt almost black beneath his white robe, alive with his telling, and eight or ten men sitting round him listening.

They came to a garden.

Palm trees with leaves like friendly elephants' trunks

waving over the wall and a whole hedge of rosemary and trumpets of tumbling lilies on a giant bush and everywhere small mosaic ponds with fountains playing, and a breeze from the Atlas mountains, clattering the heavy leaves, drums to the birds' song, and butterflies in the honeysuckle.

He bent her back across a giant boulder, with one arm behind her back so she couldn't move and had no idea what he was going to do next, so she felt a kind of weakening and a going-with-the-wind, a kind of exquisite fatality, a letting go. She thought he might easily kill her – he showed all the signs of hysteria, he wasn't easy. No, she had given the wrong impression – if it was one of easy confidence – oh no. Sometimes she thought he was madder than she was – and hungry in his madness. Whereas she grew numb and ceased to care, he grew wild with a giant appetite, sat up all night eating, made love to her for two or three hours at a time till she was passing out with exhaustion and he had still not finished with her, and he tried to make her dig it all. Turn on to the world, but she didn't know that she had the stomach for it – and sometimes she thought he didn't either but that he forced himself to it, threatened himself with eternal extinction if he refused to live now ...

So he was always at her with his constant need for never-ending nerve-racking hungry attention, his sudden bouts of marvellous laughter when his eyes went all soft and grey and he became so lovely, so approachable and exquisite.

Then he'd withdraw and walk away into the trees without saying anything and I'd walk behind him at a total loss, wondering what on earth to do and then he'd catch hold of me, clinging and kissing me with such force – not even sexually but just with a hot electric current of energy – that each kiss was an explosion of contact hissing on my skin.

So the whole relationship was out of my experience and my control – I didn't care even, my terror that he would kill me just passed like a thrilling wind blowing me out of the world.

Oh, the exquisite memory of that sheer terror when he put his fingers round my neck. Oh, kill me, take me away with you to where there'll be no resistance and I'll have no choice – I can't bear this agonizing choice.

And she remembers the same weakening release when she is lying on her bed and her little boys jump on her, crowding on to her, the baby pulling her hair and dribbling on her face and Seth sticking his tongue in her mouth, and the strength goes out of her, her strength drains into their demanding, devouring bodies like milk from her breasts, till she no longer exists, and as she is devoured she feels the exquisite release – the unbelievable sweetness of death.

He kept me very close, he never let me move more than an inch away and then he swam into my body on the crest of a wave, his sweat spraying over my neck and blinding my eyes.

'Come on, give me your body. That's right.' She was hot, he was soaking. The rigid stiffness of her body slowly melted as she moved. Ah oh, slowly melted – molten, rended backwards, and came alive.

'Come on,' he says, 'give, give ... '

Slowly her aching exhaustion faded and she began to sleep, thick heavy open-aired sleep. Morning, noon and night lying on a rug under a eucalyptus, her feet stuck into a bush of rosemary, the warm air stroking her cheeks and leaves falling unexpectedly on to her body. Nothing could wake her.

They were in Fez, camping on a hill overlooking the Medina. Dogs barked, people shouted their bargains or called to prayer on a trumpet, birds sang, but there were no cars – instead, the smell of horse or mule dung – and no aeroplanes in the sky. It was this machineless world that was so much easier to deal with – she felt her senses responding to its beauty, its realness, as her body had responded to the dance of the Arab – it was legs and shoulders and neck and belly she had found, singing to his tune, her bare feet slapping on the tiled floor, leaping to his leaps, bounding to his bounds – oh wind, that shakes my body free.

Here everybody walks slowly, all walk slowly, eating and talking as they go, as if the walk too were an important part of their life and not something to be mindlessly scurried through between one cup of tea and another. There is so much to look at: the tiny brown bird in the bamboo cage hanging on the red shutter, Fez in the early morning bathed in mist and sunlight. What the first traveller to the East must have seen. The cocks crowing, singing in a chant, not like the cocks in an English farmyard – aggressive and insistent – but testing their different notes in a triumph of early morning sweetness. Even the dogs bark more laconically.

The town in the evening so alive, so delicious, so rich with smells and people. I give a little girl some money and she hurtles off down the road with it tightly clutched in her tiny hand and three little boys hurtling after her. Her name is Zara and she is beautiful with henna-red hair.

To cease the struggle, quietly gently to be – gently quietly to love, let it come, let the feelings come, be as mystical as you like – be anything but just stop being so terrified.

Dearest Ricci,

Here I am on another continent. Things you say to me in passing always change my life, last time we met and you showed me your first miniature iris you said, 'I've never believed in too much planning to make it perfect – of course you've got to experiment a bit – but mainly it's a matter of living out the life you have.'

Now I am here, being still and feeling the foreign warmth and smells and realizing there really is no escape, and that is what you were saying – there is only now and you can only choose to confront it or turn your back on it. If you choose to confront it with all its agony and conflict, it's possible; if you turn your back on it you hate it and it's intolerable.

But it's all there is, this here and now – and the only solution is love and fascination, because fascinating it is. But avoid weariness. When the last anguish is shed there is truly nothing left and it is this, above all, that is appalling about old age – the loss of ability to see and the loss of energy to confront – and sometimes I feel old and this frightens me – Is this why I ran away? I don't really know, because in the end I knew nothing – it was as if I had gone blind and deaf and dumb – but here I can see things again. Here people seem to stay so close, babes to their mothers, houses to each other, people to people and donkeys and animals. At night the travelling men sleep beside their donkeys.

Near by there is a woman sitting against the wall with one small child on either side and a third across her lap …

Near the gate, the man selling Coca-Cola from a giant

fridge was sitting on the ground chopping kif on a tiny wooden board – his eyes peeped over the top of his counter at Maro. A small girl stood in the dust crying because her knickers had fallen down. Maro went over to her and pulled them up. The little girl stopped crying and stared hard at Maro.

What terrified her was that if he died, what would she do – how could she confront, accept, live through the fact of his death? She knew that a hundred strong men would have to hold down her agony, they would have to put hundred-pound weights on her arms and legs and bind her with thick ropes. And then what would she do with his body?

And then what about those dear little boys – what should she do with them? It occurred to Maro that the most loathsome action a woman can ever take is to abandon her children.

* * *

We went to the pictures in a tiny cinema. When we came out he said, 'Did you see their faces – well, that's what love is, just endless torture.'

Later we lay in the sleeping-bag, the night above full of stars. He sucked his cough sweets noisily beside me. And then he turned towards me, his body naked, heavy, crushing me. Biting my face, boring into me, shattering me till, broken open, I respond, my teeth on his mouth and fingers in his hair.

But he is so wild and heavy, twisting her limbs around his neck and holding her down with his teeth, till the pain hits her and she leaps back into herself, closing up tight away from him, retreating up into her head away from her body. She grows cold. He stops.

'I'm sorry, it was like a fairy story, I was being crushed and eaten by a great heavy bear ... '

'But I can't be loving and gentle all the time.'

'It was too much for me ... '

'I suppose I want a she-bear ... I want to open you up and turn you into a she-bear – to pour all my anger into you and for you to absorb it all and give me back your own.'

'But I just get sad ... '

'So you want a lover to help you keep your blanket of insulation from feeling, from people, from the harshness of the world? But I want to rip it from you.'

'I don't trust you not to kill me ... '

'That's because you don't trust yourself ... Listen to your feelings and trust them a little ... '

And Maro looked at his face almost black in the starlight, and yet broad and beautiful, and she put out her hand to touch it and as she touched his cheek it turned to dust in her hand and she looked upon his skull. And she screamed out into the night.

Later she slept and dreamt again she had multiple sclerosis and was totally paralysed from the neck down. Beside her sat a nurse feeding her Ovaltine through a plastic tube – the nurse smiled and Maro smiled back. The next morning she left Daniel and started for home.

They were going on a picnic, just twelve of them and three nurses, and Maro and the children.

Jack and Mike, the male nurses, loaded the collapsible wheel-chairs into a van and the patients were helped or lifted into a small bus.

It was a fantastic July day, the sun poured through the windows turning Tim's dark blond hair to gold – Maro wanted to shout out, 'Aren't they beautiful, my children?'

Everybody was making jokes about hiking, bicycling, lavatories – guffaws of laughter erupted about the physical inadequacies. Ricci sat quietly between Seth and Tim.

Maro saw Jack and Mike look at her with approval – not only young and lovely, but here she was on the picnic ... Ricci was lucky ... Had they noticed she hadn't been to the hospital for two months, she wondered ...

And if they knew I'm only really here because I can't escape my need for their approval. So I have returned to live in a cardboard way, mechanical, unable to live any other – like a shopping list – never spontaneous or natural, nothing alive and almost nothing good. Responsible and owing nobody nothing, but generous, warm, really loving – no never, never. So here I am zealously following my duties because duty is at least a way of life.

She felt a damp warmth seeping through her thigh. She touched Jonny's trousers but it wasn't him, it was Miss Edwin, Miss Diving Dolly Edwin on her other side, was was peeing on the green plastic seat and as she peed, a larger and larger warm stream flowed towards Maro while blue-eyed Miss Edwin stared out of the window at enormous oaks and beeches through a haze of dust.

'Ah, Miss Edwin,' she thought, 'if only I could lose my body too – then perhaps I could get really close to him ... and what do I care for my body ...

* * *

That time when it froze in the night and there was an inch of hard crisp snow on the ground and we pulled the sledge out across the meadow, the cold on their cheeks, the little boys, red faces and red hands, their screams of delight as the sledge swooped down the hill. But surely you had to have a body for this perfect delight? It couldn't be done with just a mind. And that day we took bread and cheese – a perfect October day – and walked up the hill and ate it sitting under a hedge. It was so warm we lay back in the grass with tits in the bushes over our heads, the sun on my cheeks and my heart rising like a bird. Wasn't this somehow connected with the body? Perhaps it is my mind I would do best to lose.

* * *

They had arrived at a glade in the woods. Some people were meeting them. The boys tumbled out.

Ah, it was beautiful – everywhere bluebells and tiny blades of lush grass beneath the trees. They were on the edge of a park; in the distance was a fifteenth-century manor house.

Tim and Seth disappeared into some bracken, Jonny struggling behind, shouting at them to wait for him.

Mike and Jack lifted Ricci down and put him in his wheel-chair. Maro pushed him along the track – he wanted to see the plants.

'Stop, Maro,' he kept calling, and then he would bend low, till his head rested on his knees, to get a better view of the ground.

Maro took off her shoes and put them in the chair beside Ricci. Now the cool ground was beneath her feet …

My mistake has been fear, lack of courage to recognize my own position and make it clear to others what my true needs are. No, always I have gone about things by cunning lies – now is the time to drop that, to be brave enough to penetrate to the meanest greediest depths of my soul.

'Ricci, I want to run, I want to leave you here and run … '

'No, Maro, push me … please.'

'But I don't want to spend my life pushing you around … I want to be real … '

'This is real … lean on me.'

'How can I lean on you – you with your Jilly and your garden?'

'Hit me if you hate me, Maro.'

She let go of the chair and with her hand and all her strength hit him across the head – first one side and then the other. He winced, his white cheek broke into red mottles. Suddenly he started to laugh. He laughed and laughed. Maro, amazed, started laughing too.

'Poor Maro, I've got it made: plump Jilly to wash me,

my exquisite trough garden, friends to come and talk, and now my stereo with the ear-phones. You haven't used them yet have you, they're magnificent, you really hear the music inside your head ... Wow, what an experience ... Maro, come here, I love you ... '

Someone was calling them to eat. A trestle-table had been laid out and piled with food. The children were already there, tucking in and being stroked and kissed by all who were mobile enough to stroke and kiss. Miss Edwin sat aloof as usual, the far-away look in her eyes and in her lap a bunch of primroses somebody had picked for her. Miss Edwin, you never pretend.

Why did I always have to pretend – the hard work of pretending – I never thought that you were allowed to live by real feelings – feel what you felt – tell what you felt ... Always escape, try, try not to feel. Feeling meant pain, agony, feelings were to be avoided at all costs. So love is wonderful while it sticks to some idea of a romance in a novel, but when it gets out of control, Christ ... He said to me, 'You're a liar and a coward.'

'Yes,' I said, 'yes, yes, yes.'

'Ricci,' Maro said looking at him, 'I liked hitting you.'

I yearned in some secret part of me to have a relationship where everything was shared, close, close as D said, 'It should be ALL Love, Love, Love,' and yet I was unable to trust myself or anyone else enough to give anything ... Always hold back, keep in control – never let yourself go.

Maro pushed Ricci back towards the others.

And wasn't she right in a way? She had seen people who were bold or stupid enough to let themselves go and hadn't they ended badly?

Women heavy, taken to drink, loud-mouthed, cynical,

vulgar and undignified. At least there was a dignity about her escape – or was there? Wouldn't it be more dignified to live out her miseries – hadn't she always been drawn to those who did – envious?

'Be stoical,' Ricci had once said to her, and that's what she'd always been – but was this really right – because by being stoical didn't one lose sight of one's feelings altogether? Isn't being stoical in the end just being cowardly?

To sink down and expose yourself, your raw real sensitive self, to take courage and drag away the clutter, to live with a new simplicity close to myself, to my feelings, the sun, my energy near the surface to be drawn upon and then to relax, quiet, quiet inside, not restless, not preoccupied but quiet, just listening to my heartbeat.

Love spilling over, tumbling cascading like a mountain stream, a waterfall, for the baby, the stained-glass baby, his body, his lovely little body, soft skin. His face as he tottered towards her, mouth full of sausage, his hopeful optimistic expression.

Open your heart, confront the pain, the tears, the rain, the cold. Confront each day and be aware, be alive, don't try and escape but be brave. Have courage enough to live out each day, to be soft and warm and open to life. Have courage enough not to armour and be cold and hard. Have courage to feel, to grip and tangle, not to draw back in fear. It is never-ending battle, the struggle to be fully alive.

Seth says, 'I think we're really asleep and all this is a dream, and when we die we stop dreaming and come alive.'

There are a few people who really live, and they are heroes who climb mountains or paint great pictures...

but what about me ... Must I for ever live in the songs my nanny sang me.

Oh listen, little Dear-My-Soul
To the fairy voices calling ...
For the moon is high in the misty sky,
And the honey dew is falling.

If only I could marry a doctor and then when Hell's darkness tightened its black grip on my heart, he could stick tubes down my nose and pump out the poisonous bile from my stomach. And we would live in a hospital. Doctor's weren't afraid of the ill, the ugly, the mad. The way the surgeons touched Ricci's body – doctors weren't afraid of touch. Like children's, their hands were full of healing ...

Yes, it was summer now and Maro was home. And in the afternoons they could stay in the bedroom with the windows open to the damp summer afternoons and the long grass and birds outside, and the long hours on her bed with Jonny and Seth, and the time broken up by cups of tea – theirs in bottles and hers in a mug – and chocolate biscuits with the chocolate gone shiny and soft from the warm day. And so they'd lie together on the bed, perhaps Seth would tell her one of his favourite dreams – how God came on the television and asked me to show him my pee-pee – and I will laugh – 'He did, Mum, really he did, but I can't remember if it was a dream or it happened really ... '

'Ricci,' says Maro, 'I want you to come home.'

She wrote a note to Daniel.

All you accuse me of is right but you don't understand it. Some time I will try and tell you. I respect your unrequiting search after what is real and true more than anything – even if I had really loved you I wouldn't have recognized it because it would be a new feeling.

I hope I never gave you the impression the children were a burden on me – now I look back on it this was not so, they were the most real and joyful part of my existence. Sometimes on the most desolate occasions they relapsed into a wild gaiety when, late at night, the house would be filled with their laughter and their exotic untamed unweary chants – poetry brimmed from their small lips and their vibrations filled the house with life ... my heart woke up – their fantasies, their dreams, their uncaptured souls – No, they were never a burden – the burden was myself. My thick fears and heavy cluttered mind, my apathy, my rigidness, my lack of courage. Because with strength I could have taken those three babies under my arm and been the woman I needed and wanted to be and my babies would have grown up just as well. No, babies are no excuse.

And as for happiness – I know what happiness is – I have experienced it: everything glows and a faint smell of warmth comes off the grass and trees and suddenly one is there, not up in some tiny corner of one's tiny mind. But you see I am incapacitated, I can't take it and I never have been able to. I remember when I was four years old all the other children on hot summer afternoons going across the grass to the swimming-pool and I feigning ear-ache, lying in my room with the curtains drawn against the sun – they were yellow and had bees on them, but enough light came through for me to see my arm hanging heavy over the side of the bed and watch my fingers sweep and dangle against the floor, whilst in the distance I heard the splashing and merry shouts of children at play. And sometimes a tiny ray of sun would push between the curtains and if I was lucky, it might fall somewhere on my bed.